ORIORI NO UTA
Poems for All Seasons

装幀 ● 菊地信義

装画 ● 野村俊夫

写真 ● ジョニー・ハイマス（Johnny Hymas）

翻訳協力 ● 一場慎司（序文）
　　　　　● 緒方恵一（作者略歴）

Published by Kodansha International Ltd.,
17-14 Otowa 1-chome, Bunkyo-ku, Tokyo 112-8652.
No part of this publication may be reproduced
in any form or by any means without permission
in writing from the publisher.
Copyright © Ōoka Makoto 2000.
English translation copyright © Janine Beichman.
All rights reserved. Printed in Japan.

First Edition, 2000

ISBN4-7700-2380-4
00 01 02 03   10 9 8 7 6 5 4 3 2 1

折々のうた

ORIORI NO UTA
Poems for All Seasons

大岡 信[著]
ジャニーン・バイチマン[訳]

Bilingual Books

序 文

　大岡信の『折々のうた』は、日本の代表的新聞『朝日新聞』の第一面に、多少の休載はあったものの、20年以上にわたって毎日連載されてきた。1979年1月25日に始まったこのコラムはすでに5,000回を越えている。大岡さんは一つの短詩あるいは長詩からの数行をとり、作品の魅力を語り、難解な語句を解説する。その選択範囲は広く、伝統的な俳句、短歌から漢詩、沖縄のおもろ、18世紀の狂歌、西洋詩の翻訳にまで至る。大岡さんに選ばれた作者は、各時代にわたり、また翻訳作品の原作者を含めると、多くの国々に広がっている。その解説はまた、ある時は原詩のこれまで気づかれなかった側面を明らかにし、作品の鑑賞を難しくしている一語を摘出解説し、あるいはその作品を凡百の他作を越えるものにしている表現を指摘するなど、しばしば原詩と同じくらい面白い。

　1994年に出版された拙訳『折々のうた』英語版（*A Poet's Anthology*——ケイティディド・ブックス刊）の序文で、ドナルド・キーン先生は、詩歌のコラムをこれほど重視している新聞はおそらく世界のどこにも存在しないであろうと指摘している。日本では詩歌は伝統的に大衆芸術である。十七音の俳句または三十一音の短歌は、シェークスピアのソネットよりもおぼえやすく、少なくとも初心者には作りやすいように思えるであろう。日本の新聞には、ほぼ例外なく短歌・俳句欄があり、読者の投稿した作品を専門家が選定、批評してくれる。しかし大岡さんの仕事にはそれ以上のものがある。20世紀初頭、詩歌と俳句を現代に復活させた詩人兼批評家、与謝野鉄幹と正岡子規の伝統を受け継いで、大岡信は読者が詩歌を形態で分類するという表面的区分から解放され、詩歌としての根元的統一性を見るよう求める。歌人の子として生まれた大岡さんは、詩作を始めたころにはシュールレアリスムに多大の影響を受け、現在は自由詩ばかりでなく連詩を書いている。大岡さんは言う。「『折々のうた』で私が企てているのは「日本詩

PREFACE

Ōoka Makoto's *Oriori no Uta* (Poems for All Seasons) has appeared on the front page of the *Asahi Shimbun*, the leading Japanese newspaper, every day (with a few breaks) for over twenty years. Since Jan 25, 1979, Ōoka has written over 5,000 such columns. In each he chooses a short poem or a few lines from a longer one, then explains why he finds it appealing and comments on any difficult words or phrases. His selection is broad, ranging from the traditional *haiku* and *tanka*, to poetry in classical Chinese, Okinawan ritual verse, 18th century satiric verse, and poems translated from Western languages. The authors he chooses come from all periods and several countries, so he uses translations too. His comments are often as interesting as the poems themselves, revealing special aspects that others have not noticed or pinpointing just the word that makes the poem difficult, or the expression that lifts it out of the ordinary.

As Donald Keene pointed out in his preface to *A Poet's Anthology* (Katydid Books, 1994), the previous volume of my *Oriori no Uta* translations, there is probably not a newspaper anywhere else in the world that features a poetry column so prominently. In Japan, poetry has traditionally been a popular art; it is easier to remember a 17-syllable *haiku* or a 31-syllable *tanka* than a Shakepearean sonnet and, at least in the beginning, it seems easier to write them too. Almost all newspapers have *tanka* and *haiku* columns to which readers send their poems to be judged by professional poets. But Ōoka's endeavor involves something more. In the tradition of Yosano Tekkan and Masaoka Shiki, the poet-critics who at the turn of the 20th century brought the *tanka* and *haiku* into the modern age, Ōoka wants his audience to break free of the superficial distinctions that divide different poetic forms and see their underlying unity as poetry. The son of a *tanka* poet himself, he was deeply influenced by surrealism early in his career and today writes linked verse as well as free verse. "With *Oriori no Uta*," he wrote, "I planned a kind of compendium of Japanese poetry, a storehouse open to everyone, that would include

5

歌の常識」づくり。和歌も漢詩も歌謡も俳諧も今日の詩歌も、ひっくるめてわれわれの詩、万人に開かれた言葉の宝庫。この常識を、わけても若い人々に語りたい。手軽な本で。……日本の詩の歴史を、短歌、俳句、近代以降の詩という三つの分野について見るだけで足れりとしがちな世の「常識」を、私は大いに疑問とする。……私が日本の詩歌について知るところははなはだ狭くとぼしい。もし、古今の秀作をすべて網羅しようなどと考えてこの企てに乗りだしたのだったら、……たちまち挫折してしまっただろう。……代わりに、私は古今の詩句を借りてそれをあるゆるやかな連結方法によってつなぎとめながら、全体として一枚の大きな言葉の織物ができるように、それらを編んでみたいと思ったのである。」

　コラムが集積すると、大岡さんはそれを本にまとめた。新聞では一回に詩は二行、解説は180字に限定された。しかし大岡さんはそれを「限定」と考えず、「ほとんどの場合その制限内で書くことが一種の楽しみでさえあった。」と書いている。本のときは、解説に30字の増加が許されたが、大岡さんは省略をいくらか展開するにとどめ、新たな変更は行わなかった。『折々のうた』には現在では新書や文庫もあり、1992年に始まる14冊のシリーズとなっている。

　私は正岡子規の伝記を書いたときにはじめて大岡信の仕事を知った。講談社の『正岡子規全集』に子規晩年の短歌を論ずるすばらしい随筆を書いておられたからである。その後、大岡さんの能に対する関心を知った私は、私の英文による新作能 Drifting Fires を和訳してくれる人を求めて、大岡さんにうかがいをたてた。それは、ご本人は多忙にちがいないから、だれか適当な人をご存知ないかと考えてのことであった。驚いたことに、大岡さんは自分が翻訳を引き受けると言われ、私を喜ばせてくださった（その翻訳は、川村ハツエ著『能のジャポニスム』1987年、七月堂刊に原文と共に対訳形式で収録されている）。1990年に『朝日イブニングニュース』が週一回『折々のうた』の英訳を掲載すると決めたとき、大岡さんが私

poetry in Japanese and classical Chinese, folksongs and modern poetry. I wanted it to appeal above all to young people, and to be easy to read .... Japanese poetry is traditionally divided into *tanka*, *haiku*, and modern poetry, but I have deep doubts about that.... Not knowing all of Japanese poetry or even all of its best poems, I could not aspire to include all of them and so did not undertake to. Instead, I have tried to weave together verses old and new, loosely linking them in a 'tapestry of words.'"

As the columns accumulated, Ōoka published them in book form. In the newspaper, he is limited to two lines for the poetry and 180 characters for his own comments. He has not found the brevity "constraining" but, on the contrary, he writes, "I have almost always felt it a kind of pleasure to write within those restraints." In the books, allowed an extra thirty characters for his comments, he unfolded some of his elisions; otherwise, there is no change. There are now scores of volumes in various paperback editions and a fourteen volume compilation that goes up to 1992.

I first encountered Ōoka Makoto's work while writing my biography of Masaoka Shiki, for Ōoka had written a beautiful essay on the *tanka* of Shiki's last years for the Kōdansha *Masaoka Shiki Zenshū*. Later I discovered Ōoka's interest in Noh, so when I needed a translator for my English-language Noh play, *Drifting Fires*, it seemed natural to approach him. I assumed he himself was much too busy, but thought he might know someone qualified. To my surprise and delight, he offered to translate the play himself (Kawamura Hatsue, *Noh no Jyaponisumu* Shichigatsudō Press, 1987 includes the translation and the original, in bilingual format). In 1990, when the *Asahi Evening News* decided to make his column a weekly feature, Ōoka recommended me as the translator, and I have been doing a translation every week since then. For this

を翻訳者として推薦してくださり、以来私はその翻訳を続けている。本書を編むにあたっては、私がこれまでに翻訳した520余編のなかから、講談社インターナショナルの編集者が120編ほどを選び、巻末に作者の短い略歴を添えた。

　本書に収録された詩歌のうち英訳されていないものが多い。しかし、すでに英訳のあるものも、その訳に敬意をはらいつつも、すべて私が新たに英訳した。訳文はすべて大岡さんに示して承認を得た。しかし、もし翻訳に誤りがあるとすれば、それはもちろん私の責任である。本書編纂にあたって適切なアドバイスをくれた長女山本彩にも感謝したい。

　人間だれしも十年一日というわけにはいかず、私も『折々のうた』の翻訳を続けているうちに、自分の翻訳の方法が変わってきたことに気づいている。もちろん不変の要素もいくつかはある。詩歌の翻訳をする場合、私は原作のイメージの順序を保つことを試みる。同時に、意味をより明確にする目的で語句を付け加えることを避けている。これは俳句や短歌のような短詩や短い漢詩を翻訳するときについ犯しがちなことである。しかし、これは一種の水増しであり、原詩の力を薄めてしまうのである。俳句や短歌を翻訳するときには、まず私はそれぞれを17音節、31音節の英語にしようと試みる。これは音節数を保つことを最重要と考えているわけではなく、自分に推敲の材料を与えるためなのである。仕上げの段階ではいい英語にするために音節数を犠牲にすることもよくある。私は、短歌を3行で書く石川啄木を別にして、短歌はふつう5行に、俳句は3行に、その他の詩は原作の行数に合わせて翻訳することにしている。これは個人的趣味の問題であって、俳句は3行、短歌は5行と決まっているからではない。日本の詩歌には、行数を定めた定型詩という概念はなく、強調されるのは音節数である。(この点に関しては、私の書いた「短歌の翻訳:行分け」(*The Tanka Jornal*, 1993年7月号) および同シリーズの他の翻訳者の文にくわしい)。『朝日イブニングニュース』に訳すときの私は、行頭の引っこめ、大文字の使用、句読点な

volume, the editors at Kōdansha International chose about 120 from the 520 or so columns I have done until now, then added short biographies of each poet at the end.

Many of the poems included here have not been translated into English before. Even when an earlier translation exists, I have, with all due respect to earlier translators, translated anew. Each translation was shown to Ōoka for his approval, and he graciously answered many questions, but responsibility for any mistakes is, of course, mine alone. I am also grateful to my daughter Aya Yamamoto for her helpful editorial advice during the process of revising the columns to make this book.

No one stays the same for ten years, and during the time I have been translating *Oriori no Uta*, I have noticed changes in the way I translate. There are, however, some constants. In translating the poems, I always try to preserve the order of images in the original. At the same time, I avoid adding words to make the meaning clearer. Such additions are a constant temptation when dealing with minimalist forms like the *haiku*, *tanka*, and the shorter forms of classical Chinese poetry, but they are a kind of padding and cannot help but dilute the effect of the original poem. I often begin translating a *haiku* or *tanka* by aiming at 17 or 31 syllables. This is not because I think maintaining syllable count is important, but in order to give myself a form to work against. In the finished translation, syllable count is often sacrificed for the sake of pleasing English. I usually translate the *tanka* into five lines (except in the case of Ishikawa Takuboku, who used three), and *haiku* into three lines, and other poems into the number of lines their authors have used. This is a matter of personal taste, and not because I think that the *haiku* is really three lines and the *tanka* is five. The concept of a fixed number of lines is foreign to Japanese poetics; it is not the number of lines, but the number of syllables that has been stressed. (More on this topic is in my "Translating *Tanka*: Lineation," *The Tanka Journal*, July 1993, and articles by other translators in the same series.) When translating for the *Asahi Evening News*, I tend to allow some diversity in the way I indent, capitalize and punctuate the

どには多少の変化をつけている。しかし本書編集にあたって見直してみると、ページの組み方、あるいは詩をおさめるテンプレートが、もっと視覚的に統一された形態をとってもいいと思うようになった。

大岡さんの解説は会話体といえるほどの調子で書かれているので、読みやすい。『折々のうた』の翻訳を始めたとき、詩そのものより解説のほうが翻訳しやすいと考えたのはそのためであった。解説が、そこで扱われる詩作品と同じように、簡潔にして緻密かつきっちりと圧縮された批評的エッセーであるとわかるには時を要した。最初のころは、英語圏の読者が知りそうもないことがらをときどき付け加えたものである。しかし、経験を重ねるにつれ、このような挿入物は、それ自体は面白いかもしれないが、解説に詩とは無関係な情報を加え、むしろ大岡氏の洞察を弱めてしまうことに気づくようになった。そして、現在では、できるかぎり控えめで簡潔な翻訳になるように心がけている。また、絶対に必要なときに限って、大岡さんの省略したところを補うことにしている。一つ例をあげれば、万福寺（p.188）が中国の様式で建てられているという注で、この知識がないと、大岡さんが引用している田上菊舎の俳句が意味をなさなくなるのである。

解説の翻訳で最も難しいのは、しばしば最後にある、簡潔でありながら暗示に富んだ一言である。その二つの好例が、飯田蛇笏（p.186-187）と良寛（p.168-169）の作品の扱いである。この解説を、省略と含意を補って説明するならば、ぶちこわしとなるであろう。私は全体の意味をそこなわないようにしつつも、その簡潔さを保とうとつとめた。

『折々のうた』の翻訳を始めたときの私の日本詩歌の歴史の見方は直線的であった。まず『万葉集』と人麻呂、『古今集』と小野小町、紀貫之、『新古今集』と藤原俊成おびその子定家、ついで松尾芭蕉、与謝蕪村、そして正岡子規、与謝野晶子、斉藤茂吉、最後に大岡氏を含めた多くの現代詩人である。

poems. But in going over the poems for this book, I found that here, the shape of the pages—the template, in other words, within which the poem sits—encouraged a more uniform visual shape for the poems.

Ōoka's commentaries are easy to read, almost conversational in tone. Perhaps that is why, when I first began translating *Oriori no Uta*, I thought his comments easier to translate than the poems. It took me some time to realize that his comments are actually tightly compressed critical essays, as compact and dense in their own way as the poems they describe. When I first began translating the columns, I often added information that English-speaking readers could not be expected to know. As I gained experience, however, I realized that such interpolations, interesting as they might be in themselves, overloaded the commentary with information irrelevant to the poem and, paradoxically, diluted Ōoka's insights. I now aim for a minimalist style of translation which stays as much in the background as possible. Only when absolutely necessary do I introduce what Ōoka omits. One example is the information that Manpukuji (p. 189) is built in Chinese style, for without this knowledge, the poem by Tagami Kikusha that Ōoka quotes in the commentary would make no sense.

The most difficult part of translating the commentaries is the compact yet suggestive critical remarks with which they often conclude. Two good examples are in the treatment of the poems by Iida Dakotsu (pp. 186–187) and the priest Ryōkan (pp. 168–169). To translate these remarks in an explanatory way, unfolding all the elisions and implications, would ruin the effect. I tried to retain the conciseness without losing the full meaning.

When I began translating *Oriori no Uta*, my idea of the history of Japanese poetry was linear. First came the *Man'yōshū* and Hitomaro, then the *Kokinshū* with Ono no Komachi and Ki no Tsurayuki, then the *Shin Kokinshū* with Fujiwara Shunzei and his son Teika; the next important poet was Matsuo Bashō, then Yosa Buson, then came Masaoka Shiki,

『折々のうた』はもう一つの見方を示してくれる。このコラムは、しばし一つのグループを追うこともあり（たとえば子供の現代俳句や、日本語で書く台湾の人々の作品）、特定のテーマやイメージにもとづく作品を追うこともある。しかし、これらも『折々のうた』全体から見た場合、それほど多くはない。全体の印象は、その驚くほど変化に富んだ詩人たちが一堂に会しているというものである。年表や直線的な詩歌の歴史を離れて、『折々のうた』を「言葉の織物」に仕上げている「ゆるやかに連結した」糸は、E. M.フォースターの、大きな円い部屋に座をとった小説家たちが、同時に各自の作品を書いているイメージ（『小説の諸相』）を思い起こさせる。私には『折々のうた』は、そのとなりにある詩人たちの部屋のように感じられる。あるいは詩人たちは小説家と同じ部屋にずっと住んでいたが、陰にかくれていたのかもしれない。さあ、みなさん、私と一緒にこの部屋をのぞいてみようではありませんか。

　　　　　　　　　　　　　ジャニーン・バイチマン
　　　　　　　　　　　　　2000年、つくばにて

掲載作者の作品を知るには、巻末の「作者略歴」（アイウエオ順による）の、作者名のあとの頁数を参照してください。

Yosano Akiko, Saitō Mokichi, and a host of modern poets, including Ōoka himself.

Oriori no Uta added another way of seeing. The columns would sometimes follow one group of poets for a while (for example, modern *haiku* by children, or Taiwanese who write in Japanese), or present a few consecutive poems on a single theme or image. But such series are short compared to the length of the whole of *Oriori no Uta* itself; the impression remains of a tremendous variety of poets all in one place. In place of chronology and the linear image of poetic history, the "loosely linked" threads that make up *Oriori no Uta's* "tapestry of words" recall E. M. Forster's image in *Aspects of the Novel* of all novelists seated together in a large, circular room, writing their works simultaneously. I think of *Oriori no Uta* as the room for poets that lies next door. Or perhaps the poets have been there with the novelists all along, but in the shadows. Here they are, and may you enjoy them as much as I have.

Janine Beichman
Tsukuba, Japan, 2000

To locate a particular poet's work, see the page number after his or her name in the short biographies at the back, which are arranged in kana order.

折々のうた・

Oriori no Uta
Poems for All Seasons

大岡　信 [著]
Ōoka Makoto

ジャニーン・バイチマン [訳]
Janine Beichman

春のうた

SPRING POEMS

真木ふかき
Maki   fukaki

谷よりいづる
tani   yori   izuru

山水の
yamamizu no

常あたらしき
tsune   atarashiki

生命あらしめ
inochi   arashime

今井邦子
Imai Kuniko

『紫草』(昭六)所収。「真木」はすぐれた木の意で、檜・杉・槙などの良材をいった。「山水の」は、山水のように。緑なす山、その奥深い谷から湧き出る水のように、常に新しい息吹に満ちた生命をここに(私の身うちに)湧き立たせて下さい、という祈りをこめた歌。大自然の純粋な生命と人間の卑小さを対比して前者を讃える歌はよくあり、陳腐にもなり易いが、この歌は調べが張っている。

From valleys deep

with evergreens

the mountain springs arise

Let my life be as fresh forever

and as new as these

Imai Kuniko

From *Murasaki-gusa* (Purple Grasses, 1931). *Maki* "evergreens," means evergreen trees prized as tim-ber, such as cypress and cedar. *Yamamizu no,* "moun-tain springs," is short for *yamamizu no yō ni,* "like the mountain springs." The poem is a prayer: Like the water that wells up from the deep valleys in the evergreen mountains, let there well up here (within my body) a life always filled with new breath. Many poems praise nature by contrasting its purity with the pettiness of human concerns, a theme which can easily become banal; but something about this poem's ripely swelling cadence sets it apart.

身のはてを
Mi no hate wo

知らず思はず
shirazu omowazu

今日もまた
kyō mo mata

人の心の
hito no kokoro no

薄氷を踏む
usurai wo fumu

石上露子
Isonokami Tsuyuko

『石上露子集』(昭三四)所収。「明星」発表の哀切な失恋の詩「小板橋」で有名だが、実生活は、上記の集を編んだ松村緑教授の評伝が出るまでは大方謎だった閨秀歌人。熱愛した人が外国に去り、結婚した夫には徹底して自由を束縛されたという。しかも、愛する二人の男子にも先立たれた。だが師の与謝野晶子は露子を高く評価していた。目覚めた鋭い人間性観察者だったことは、上の歌に底流する現実感覚からも明らか。

Don't know, don't care where

this will take me—

Today I step out afresh

onto the thin ice

of a man's heart

Isonokami Tsuyuko

From *Isonokami Tsuyuko Shū*, 1959. A woman poet famous for "Koitabashi," a tragic poem of unrequited love that was published in *Myōjō*. Her real life story was almost completely unknown until the publication of her biography by Professor Matsumura Midori, who also edited the collection of her poetry from which this poem is taken. Matsumura tells us that Isonokami Tsuyuko passionately loved a man who left her to go abroad, and later married another who kept her in total subjection. Both of her beloved sons predeceased her. Yosano Akiko was her tanka teacher and esteemed her work highly. The sense of precise realism that underlies this poem clearly comes from an awakened and alert observer of humanity.

吾なくば
Ware nakuba

わが世もあらじ
waga yo mo araji

人もあらじ
hito mo araji

まして身を焼く
masite mi wo yaku

思もあらじ
omoi mo araji

柳原白蓮
Yanagihara Byakuren

『踏絵』(大四)所収。伯爵令嬢として生まれ、少女時代から佐佐木信綱に歌を学び、華族に嫁して離婚、大富豪と再婚するが恋人を得て婚家を去る。世の好奇の噂のまととなって実家に監禁され、のちついに恋人と同棲を果たす。明治十八年生まれの白蓮のこういう経歴は、自らの真情、女の自己解放と、社会の因襲とのあいだの闘争の連続だった。上はまだ若かりし日の歌だが、この「吾なくば」の思想は筋金入り。

If I did not exist,

my world would not exist,

he would not exist—

and then there would be no

passion to burn my soul

Yanagihara Byakuren

From *Fumie* (Treading Pictures, 1915). Born the daughter of a count, Byakuren studied tanka from girlhood with Sasaki Nobutsuna, married into another noble family, divorced and married an extremely rich man, but then fell in love with some-one else and ran away with him. As a result, she became the target of malicious gossip and was imprisoned by her family in their home. Later, she finally succeeded in marrying her lover. Born at the end of the 19th century, in 1885, Byakuren's life was a continuing battle to honor her own feelings, and for a woman's right to live freely in spite of society's strictures. This poem dates from her youth, but the thought behind the phrase "if I did not exist" shows her already-resolute will.

はるの夜の
Haru no yo no

女とは
onna to wa

我むすめ哉
waga musume kana

榎本其角
Enomoto Kikaku

『五元集』所収。「遠遊酔帰の駕(かご)のうちにて」と前書がある。其角は蕩児だった。「酒を妻つまを妾の花見哉」など、いい気なもんだといわれそうな句も作っている。師の芭蕉とはその点正反対。その其角が、まだ少女といっていい年齢のわが娘と一緒に遠出をし、大酔してかごで帰る時、ふと娘に「女」を感じてはっと驚いたさまの句である。父情は複雑、艶っぽい味もあって、春夜の句の珍品だろう。

This woman who lights

the spring night . . .

my own daughter!

Enomoto Kikaku

From *Gogenshū*. The preface is: "Returning home drunk by palanquin, after an excursion." Kikaku led a dissolute life. Some of his haiku make him sound quite pleased with himself: "Liquor my wife, /my wife a concubine/—that's flower-viewing!" (*sake wo tsuma/tsuma wo mekake no/hanami kana*). In this respect, he was the mirror opposite of his master, Bashō. Kikaku had gone on an excursion with his daughter, who was not even old enough to be married, and as he rode home in the palanquin with her, drunk as a lord, he suddenly noticed her femaleness with surprise. This poem, with its evocation of the erotic aspect of complex paternal feelings, is a rarity among haiku on the topic of a spring night.

みづうみの
Mizu-umi   no

氷は解けて
kōri wa   tokete

なほ寒し
nao   samushi

三日月の影
Mikazuki no kage

波にうつろふ
nami ni   utsurou

島木赤彦
Shimagi Akahiko

『太虚集』(大十三)所収。「諏訪湖畔」と小題にある。現在も同じ場所にあるが、赤彦の家は信州の諏訪湖を斜めに前方に見おろせる位置にあった。彼は湖水を愛して数々の秀歌をのこしたが、中でも一、二を争うのがこの歌だろう。張りつめていた氷は少しずつ解けはじめたが、寒さはなお厳しい。空にかかった三日月が、糸のように繊細な姿を湖の波に映してたゆたっている。光ともいえぬ光を発して静まる、その幽遠の影。

The ice on the lake

is melting but

it's still cold

The crescent moon's light

flickers over the waves

Shimagi Akahiko

From *Taikyoshū* (The Great Void, 1924), this tanka
is titled "On the Banks of Lake Suwa." Akahiko's
house was (and still remains) on a piece of land
looking down diagonally on Lake Suwa. This is
one of the very best of the many excellent poems he
left about the lake he loved. The ice that had completely covered the lake has begun to melt but it is
still bitterly cold. The crescent moon hangs in the
sky, thin as a thread. Its reflection on the waves gives
off a shimmering light that can hardly be called
light—quiet, and of immeasurable depth.

春の岬旅のをはりの鷗どり
Haru no misaki tabi no owari no kamomedori

浮きつつ遠くなりにけるかも
ukitsutsu tōku narinikeru kamo

三好達治
Miyoshi Tatsuji

　第一詩集『測量船』(昭五)巻頭を飾った短歌形式の二行詩。昭和二年四月、伊豆湯ケ島に転地療養中だった親友の作家梶井基次郎を見舞ったあと、下田から駿河湾を横切って清水まで渡ったときの船中の作らしい。岬の波間に浮くかもめが、視野をしだいに遠ざかってゆく。それは言いかえれば自分が後ろ向きに陸地から遠ざかってゆくことだ。ひとつの「旅のをはり」は次の旅の始まりなのである。

The cape in spring—at journey's end

a seagull, floating, moves far off into the distance

Miyoshi Tatsuji

This two-line poem, which in terms of syllable count is a tanka, opened *Sokuryōsen* (1930), Miyoshi's first collection of poetry. In April 1927 he visited his close friend, the writer Kajii Motojirō, who was convalescing at Yugashima in Izu, and this poem was apparently written on his way back, as he crossed Suruga Bay from Shimoda to Shimizu. A seagull bobbing on the waves arround the cape moves farther and farther away as he watches. In other words, the poet is facing backwards, watching the land as it recedes into the distance. One "journey's end" is the beginning of another.

大和は
Yamato *wa*

国の真秀ろば
kuni *no* *mahoroba*

畳なづく
Tatanazuku

青垣
aokaki

山籠れる
yama *komoreru*

大和しうるはし
Yamato *shi* *uruwashi*

古事記歌謡
Kojiki kayō

　古代伝説の悲劇の皇子倭 建 命が伊勢の能煩野で絶命する時、故郷をしのんで歌ったものという。「真秀ろば」はマホラ、マホラマと同じで、すぐれた所の意。一首、大和は陸の秀でた所、重なりあう青い垣根のような山々に抱かれた大和こそ、げに美わしい所、という意味だが、実際は皇子の事蹟とは無関係に、国見の儀式の時歌われた国ぼめの歌だろうという。しかし、非運の皇子のいまわのきわの懐郷の歌として読むとき、この歌はまことにあわれ深い。

Yamato is

the best of lands

Ringed by

green fences

by mountains enfolded

Yamato the beautiful!

Kojiki song

When the tragic prince of ancient legend, Yamato Takeru, died on the Nobo Plain in Ise, he is said to have recited this poem of longing for his homeland. *Mahoroba*, which is the same as *mahora* and *maho-rama* means "a superb place." The poem says that Yamato is such a place and, encircled as it is by rings of mountains as if by green fences, it is truly beautiful. In fact, though, it probably bore no relation to the facts of Yamato Takeru's life, but was a poem of praise sung during the *kunimi*, or "land-viewing" religious rite. And yet, when read as a poem of nostalgia for his homeland by this ill-fated prince just before he died, this poem is deeply moving.

わがこころ
Waga kokoro

しづかならざる
shizuka narazaru

ときにきて
toki ni kite

語りつくせよ
kataritsukuse yo

遠き世のこと
tōki yo no koto

山中智恵子
Yamanaka Chieko

『星肆』(昭五九)所収。「語りつくせよ」と呼びか
けられているのは作者の亡き夫である。「この夜
のねむりの底にいつかきてやさしき死者ときみな
りたまふ」。作者は三十数年間共に生きた夫を失
い、その後ごく短い期間におびただしい数の哀傷
の歌を詠んだ。上の歌はじかに悲嘆を詠んでいな
いが、それだけに優しい詠風にこもる哀しみが胸
に響く。歌がいわば死者との合作になっているの
である。

At times when my heart

is unquiet

come and tell me

every single thing you have to tell

about that long-lost world

Yamanaka Chieko

From *Seishi*, 1984. The poet is speaking to her dead husband. "At the bottom of this night's sleep/you will come sometime,/become one of the gentle dead" (*kono yoru no/nemuri no soko ni/itsuka kite/yasashiki shisha to/kimi naritamō*). Shortly after the poet lost her husband, with whom she had lived for thirty years, she wrote a tremendous number of poems of mourning in a very short time. The poem above does not express her grief directly, but the grief hidden within its quiet tenderness is all the more moving for that. The poem turns, as it were, into a collaboration with the man it mourns.

浅みどり
Asamidori

花も ひとつに
hana mo hitotsu ni

かすみつつ
kasumitsutsu

おぼろに見ゆる
oboro ni miyuru

春の夜の月
haru no yo no tsuki

菅原孝標女
Sugawara Takasue no Musume

『新古今集』巻一春上。作者は『更級日記』の著者で、この歌も日記にある。祐子内親王の御殿で、男女入りまじって春秋の比較論に興じた時、秋が好きだという人が多かったので、彼女は春に肩入れしてこれを詠んだ。秋はすべてが色鮮やか、一つ一つがくっきりしている。逆に春は、薄緑の空も桜の花も春夜の月も、すべてがおぼろに霞んで溶け合う。そこがいいと主張する。要するに日本列島の一特徴である、豊かな水蒸気の讃美なのだが。

The blossoms too are

pale green, one with the mist

in its rising—

and this spring night the moon

shows itself as in a dream

The daughter of Sugawara no Takasue

From *Shinkokinshū*, Book I, Spring 1. The author also wrote *Sarashina Nikki*, and this poem appears there as well. At the palace of Princess Yūshi some men and women were once amusing themselves by debating the merits of spring and autumn. The majority came down on the side of autumn, so this poet wrote a poem in favor of spring. In autumn, everything is bright and stands out brilliantly, but in spring it is the reverse. The light green of the sky, the cherry blossoms and the moon at night melt together in the all-encompassing, pale green mist. This, she asserts, is just what is good about spring. In a sense, this is a hymn of praise to the abundant mists and haze that are distinctive features of the Japanese archipelago.

紙雛や
Kamibina ya

恋したさうな
koi shitasō na

顔ばかり
kao bakari

正岡子規
Masaoka Shiki

『寒山落木』所収、明治二十六年作。雛祭りの起源は古い。みそぎや祓に用いた紙の人形、つまり形代から始まったといわれる。近世以前は、形代と同じように、節句がすむと川や海へ流したものである。紙雛はその意味で最も原初的な形をとどめたものだろう。雛祭りの句は古来たくさんあるが、子規の句は、ざっくばらんな口調の中に、愛らしくもまた物言いたげな表情の紙雛への親しみが溢れていて異色。

Paper dolls—

they all look as if

they want to be in love

Masaoka Shiki

A haiku of 1893 from *Kanzan Rakuboku* (Cold Mountain, Bare Trees). The Dolls' Festival (March 3) is ancient in origin. Its dolls probably originated from the paper dolls used in Shinto prayers and purification ceremonies. In medieval times, the festival dolls, like Shinto ceremonial ones, were thrown into the river or the ocean after the holiday was over. This similarity suggests that paper dolls for the Dolls' Festival were probably the earliest form. Among the many haiku, traditional and modern, about the Dolls' Festival, Shiki's is rather unusual. The language and tone are straightforward and unadorned, but there is a kind of overflowing affection for the dolls, whose captivating expressions suggest they would speak if they could.

樹脂の香に　朝は悩まし
Jushi　no　ka　ni　asa　wa　nayamashi

うしなひし　さまざまのゆめ、
Ushinaishi　samazama　no　yume,

森竝は、風に鳴るかな
Morinami　wa　kaze　ni　naru　kana

中原中也
Nakahara Chūya

『山羊の歌』(昭九)所収。「朝の歌」と題する文語
十四行詩第三連。作者自らが認めた詩的出発の作
だった。当時作者は十九歳。一編全体は、寝床で
目覚めたばかりの少年の視覚・聴覚・嗅覚にとら
えられた外界の印象をえがきつつ、早くも少年詩
人を染め上げている生の憂愁を歌っている。それ
でも「樹脂の香に　朝は悩まし」。若い生命力の
自己主張がそこにはあった。

Morning aches with resin's scent

Various lost dreams,

Forests whistle in the wind

Nakahara Chūya

From *Yagi no Uta* (Goat Songs, 1935). The third stanza of a fourteen-line poem in the literary language called "Asa no Uta" (Morning Song). The author himself saw this work as his poetic beginning. When he wrote it he was 19. The poem as a whole depicts a young man lying in bed, just awake, and the sights, sounds and smells that come to him from the outer world. It is permeated with the melancholy that already identified this young poet. And yet he writes "Morning aches with resin's scent," a line which has the self-assertive energy of youth.

核弾頭
Kakudantō

五万個秘めて
gomanko　　　*himete*

藍色の
ai-iro　　*no*

天空に浮く
tenkū　*ni*　*uku*

われらが地球
warera　　*ga*　*chikyū*

加藤克巳
Katō Katsumi

『加藤克巳全歌集』（昭六〇）所収。大正四年京都府生まれの作者は、昭和十二年大学在学中に第一歌集『螺旋階段』を出した。当時の「まつ白い腕が空からのびてくる抜かれゆく脳髄のけさの快感」のような歌は、大正末以来の新感覚派文学に近い。斬新な感覚を追う態度は、上のような最近作まで一貫する。科学雑誌のイラスト画面を見るようだ。一種の哀感が漂う所が、短歌的といえばいえようか。

50,000 nuclear warheads

tucked away, it drifts

in indigo space:

our

earth

Katō Katsumi

From *Katō Katsumi Zenkashū*, 1985. Born in Kyoto in 1915, Katsumi published his first collection of tanka in 1937, while still in college. In such poems as "A pure white arm/stretches down from the sky. /My brain unravels/in morning ecstasy" (*masshiroi/ ude ga sora kara/nobite kuru/nukareyuku nōzui no/ kasa no kaikan*) he showed his affinity for the New Sensationalist novelists of the 1920s. His pursuit of fresh sensation has continued with his most recent works, like this one. It is like looking at an illustration in a science magazine, but the image is permeated by a pathos characteristic of the tanka.

私の耳は貝のから
Watashino mimi wa kai no kara

海の響をなつかしむ
umi no hibiki wo natsukashimu

堀口大學訳、コクトー
Horiguchi Daigaku *Jean Cocteau*

　訳詩集『月下の一群』(大十四)所収。二行詩。題は「耳」。この訳詩集の出現は当時の詩界に鮮烈な感銘を与え、昭和時代に入っての新世代の詩の形成に大きな影響を与えた。明治期からすでに知られていた十九世紀の西欧詩人らと並んで、とくに二十世紀フランスの新詩を多く紹介した。コクトーもその一人で、「耳」はとりわけ愛誦された。耳と貝がらの形態上の暗合が開く大きな海への扉。翻訳であることを忘れさせる日本語の、自然で高雅な美しさ。

My ears are seashells

They remember the ocean's echoes

Horiguchi Daigaku's translation of
Jean Cocteau

From *Gekka no Ichigun* (A Gathering Beneath the Moon, 1925). Publication of this collection of translations sent shock waves through the world of poetry and played an important part in the formation of Shōwa period poetry. Together with 19th century European and American poets known from the Meiji period, it introduced many new 20th century French poets, including Cocteau, whose "Ears" (the title of this poem) won great popularity. The coincidence in form between ears and seashells opens a door to the wide sea. The natural beauty and grace of the Japanese makes the reader forget it is a translation.

不来方のお城の草に寝ころびて
Kozukata no oshiro no kusa ni nekorobite

空に吸はれし
sora ni suwareshi

十五の心
Jūgo no kokoro

石川啄木
Ishikawa Takuboku

『一握の砂』(明四三)所収。「十五の心」を文字通りにとれば、啄木は明治三十三年十五歳、盛岡中学三年生だった。五年生の秋、あと半年で卒業という時期に謎めいた中退をする彼の、これはまだ夢多き少年の日の回想的自画像。「不来方」は南部藩二十万石の城跡で、現盛岡市岩手公園。「空に吸はれし」は実感そのものだろう。「教室の窓より遁げてただ一人かの城址に寝に行きしかな」。

Sprawled out on the grass

at Kozukata Castle, sucked up

into the sky—My heart at fifteen

Ishikawa Takuboku

From *Ichiaku no Suna* (A Handful of Sand, 1910). Taken literally, the last line means 1900, when Takuboku was 15 and a third-year student at Morioka Middle School. In the autumn of his fifth year, with only a half year before graduation, he withdrew, for reasons still unclear. But this is a nostalgic self-portrait of himself as a young man still full of dreams. Kozukata was the ruins of the castle of the 200,000-*koku* fief of Nambu Han; today it is Iwate Park in Morioka City. "I was sucked up into the sky" must be exactly what he felt. He also wrote, "I fled out of the classroom window/and went to sleep all alone/in those castle ruins" (*Kyōshitsu no mado yori nigete/tada hitori/kano shiro-ato ni ne ni yukishi kana*).

冬眠より
Tōmin yori

醒めし蛙が
sameshi kaeru ga

残雪の
zansetsu no

うへにのぼりて
ue ni noborite

体を平ぶ
karada wo hirabu

斎藤茂吉
Saitō Mokichi

『白き山』（昭二四）所収。明治十五年山形県生ま
れ、昭和二十八年没の歌人。第二次大戦末期東京
から故郷へ疎開した茂吉は、敗戦翌年の早春、最
上川べりにある大石田の地に移り、なお一年余り
疎開独居生活を続けた。これは昭和二十二年早春
の歌。彼は握り飯をさげて最上川のほとりを歩き
廻るのを日常としていた。結句の「体を平ぶ」と
いう的確な表現が、歌全体を引き締めると同時に
開放している。腕の冴えに一分の隙もない。

Woken from winter sleep,

the frogs ascend

the last thin layer

of snow and

spread their bodies flat

Saitō Mokichi

From *Shirokiyama* (White Mountains, 1949). A tanka poet who was born in Yamagata Prefecture in 1882 and died in 1953. Mokichi was evacuated from Tokyo to his original home in the closing days of World War II, and stayed on after the war's end, moving in early spring of the next year to the Ōishida region near the Mogami River. There he lived alone for over a year. This poem dates from early spring of 1947, when Mokichi was in the habit of taking his lunch and walking about near the Mogami River. The precision of the last line, "spread their bodies flat," pulls the whole poem together and at the same time opens it up. The mastery of craft is absolute.

てふてふが一匹韃靼海峡を渡つて行つた。

Chōchō　ga　ippiki　Dattan　Kaikyō　wo　watatte　itta.

安西冬衛
Anzai Fuyue

　詩集『軍艦茉莉』(昭四)の「春」と題する有名
な一行詩。作者は現代詩のすぐれた先駆者で、大
正末期の新散文詩運動により、現代詩に大きな影
響を与えた。韃靼海峡は間宮海峡(タタール海峡)
の古称。「てふてふ」は蝶々の古いかなづかいで、
萩原朔太郎も好んで用いた。蝶の飛びかたが目に
見えるようだからである。生まれてまもない蝶が
ただ一匹で海峡を大陸目指して渡っていった。そ
こに「春」そのものを見たのだ。韃靼の音と字が
効果的である。

A single butterfly crossed the Tatar Strait.

Anzai Fuyue

A famous one-line poem called "Spring," from the collection *Gunkan Mari*, 1929. The author, one of the pioneers of modern poetry, had tremendous influence on poetry of the 1930s on through his central role in the poetic prose movement of the late Taishō period. Dattan Kaikyō is the old Japanese name for the Tatar Straits, now called Mamiya Kaikyō. *Chōchō*, "butterfly," is written in the old way, as てふてふ, which Hagiwara Sakutarō also preferred. This is because the unvocalized sound *te-fu te-fu* brings the way the butterfly flies clearly before the eyes. A just-born butterfly crosses the Tatar Strait from Sakhalin, headed towards the mainland of Asia. In it, the poet saw spring itself, and so he named the poem. The harsh sound and the look of the characters for Dattan (the radical for "leather" suggesting saddles, horses and their fearsome riders, the Tartars) are quite effective.

ねがはくは
Negawaku *wa*

花のもとにて
hana no moto ni te

春死なむ
haru shinamu

その如月の
sono kisaragi no

望月のころ
mochizuki no koro

西行法師
Saigyō Hōshi

　『新古今集』雑下。西行の作中特に有名な歌だが、『新古今集』完成の中途で切り出し（削除）措置を受け、異本にのみ残された。「如月の望月のころ」は二月十五日（満月）をいう。太陽暦では三月末に当たる。西行の熱愛した桜の花盛りの時期に当たるが、また釈尊入滅の日でもある。出家の身として、とりわけその日に死にたいという願いをこめた歌だが、驚いたことに、彼は願った通り、河内の弘川寺で、建久元年二月十六日に没した。

Let me die in the spring

beneath

the cherry blossoms

in the Second Month

when the moon is full

Saigyō Hōshi

Shinkokinshū, Miscellaneous 2. This is one of Saigyō's most famous poems, but during the process of compilation it was removed from the *Shinkokinshū* and remained only in a variant edition. *Kisaragi no mochizuki no koro* means the full moon of the fifteenth day of the second lunar month, which corresponds to late March in the solar calendar. This would be the peak of the cherry blossoms that Saigyō loved so much, as well as the day of the Buddha's death and entrance into nirvana. It was natural for Saigyō, who was a Buddhist monk, to hope to die on that day, but surprisingly enough, he actually did die on the sixteenth day of the second lunar month, 1190.

顔じゆうを
Kao-jū *wo*

蒲公英にして
tanpopo *ni* *shite*

笑ふなり
warau *nari*

橋　閒石
Hashi Kanseki

『和栲』(昭五八) 所収。京大英文科を出たのち中
学、高商、女子大などで長年教壇に立つ英文学者
でもあった。「俳人」の名よりは「俳諧師」の名
の方が似合いそうな作風で、連句作者でもあった。
晩年とみに愛好者がふえ、名声高かったが、余裕
と笑いの世界に出没し、自在の境地を開いた点、
貴重な現代の「俳」の人だった。「かたつむり濡
れ一隅を照らしをり」。平成四年、八十九歳で没
した。

A whole face

in laughter becomes

a dandelion

Hashi Kanseki

From *Nigitae*, 1983. This poet, who graduated from the English department of Kyoto University, was also a scholar of English literature whose long teaching career spanned a middle school, a commercial high school, and a women's college. His style makes one want to call him a practitioner of the old *haikai*, rather than a haiku poet, and he also composed linked verse. In his later years, he had many devoted readers and became quite well known. His favorite haunt was the world of play and laughter, and for this, and the fact that he built his own sphere of freedom, he deserves to be seen as one of the contemporary masters of the kind of humor traditionally associated with the haiku. "Damp snail/lights up/the corner." (*katatsumuri/nure ichigū wo/terashiori*). Kanseki died in 1992 at the age of 89.

玉藻なす
Tamamo　nasu

汝が黒髪を
na　ga　kurokami　wo

手に纏きて
te　ni　makite

暁の渚に
ake　no　nagisa　ni

立ちなげくかも
tachinageku　kamo

谷川健一
Tanikawa Kenichi

『海の夫人』(平元)所収。著名な民俗学者による
六十二首連作「海の夫人」より。彦火火出見尊の
妃豊玉姫は、産屋が完成せぬうちに産気づき、巨
大なワニの姿に戻った所を夫にのぞき見されたた
め、恥じ怒って海へ去った。いわゆる他界妻の悲
恋物語だが、作者は深い愛着をこめてこれを詠ん
でいる。上は妻が去った後の情景とみえるがそう
ではない。夫が、妻のいとしさに堪えず渚に立っ
て嘆いているのである。

Your black hair

like precious seaweed

I wind about my wrist

and sighing stand

upon the dawning shore

Tanikawa Kenichi

From *Umi no Fujin* (Wife from the Sea, 1980). Part of the 62-poem tanka sequence "Wife from the Sea." The poet, a well-known ethnologist, was inspired by a legend in the *Kojiki*. Princess Toyotamahime, wife of Prince Hikohohodemi, realized she was about to give birth before the parturition hut was complete and reverted to her original shape of a giant crocodile. But when her husband stole a glance at her, she was so ashamed and angry that she returned to the sea. This is the familiar tragic love story of a supernatural wife from another world, but the poet has poured his heart into it. The poem seems to take place after the wife's return to the sea, but actually does not. The husband, unbearably in love, stands on the beach overwhelmed with emotion.

白鳥は
Shiratori wa

哀しからずや
kanashikarazu   ya

空の青
sora no ao

海のあをにも
umi no   ao   ni mo

染まずただよふ
somazu   tadayou

若山牧水
Wakayama Bokusui

　早大英文科卒業の年自費出版した第一歌集『海の声』（明四一）所収。「幾山河」の歌もこれに収める。「白鳥」はここではカモメ。平福百穂筆の歌集表紙絵も、この歌による図柄だった。空や海の青に鳥の白を対照させ、広大な自然の中に生きる海鳥の、また作者自身の若い孤愁を哀傷する。現代短歌が避ける「空の青海のあを」のような単純なくり返しが、牧水の歌ではみごとに生かされて感情を流露させた。

White bird,

are you not sad?

You drift, never dyed

by the blue of the sea

or the sky's azure

Wakayama Bokusui

From *Umi no Koe* (Sea Voices, 1908), Bokusui's first volume of tanka, published privately the year he graduated from the English Literature Department of Waseda University. The famous poem beginning *"Iku yamakawa"* (How many mountains and rivers) is in the same volume. "White bird" means a seagull here. The cover illustration by Hirafuku Hyakusui was based on this poem. Contrasting the white of the bird with the blue of the sea and sky, the poet grieves over the bird, alive in the midst of nature's vastness, and over his own youthful loneliness. Today tanka poets avoid repetitions like *"sora no ao umi no ao"* (literally, "the blue of the sky, the blue of the sea")* but in Bokusui's poems they work wonderfully to express feeling.

*I have translated the first *"ao"* as "blue" and the second as "azure" because the first is written with a *kanji* while the second is in *hiragana*.—Tr.

廻る杖は空を飛びて
Meguru　tsue　wa　sora　wo　　　tobite

初月かと疑ふ
mikazuki　ka　to　utagau

奔る毬は地を転びて
Hashiru　mari　wa　chi　wo　marobite

流星に似る
ryūsei　ni　niru

嵯峨天皇
Saga Tennō

『経国集』巻十一。「早春打毬を観る」と題する
七言律詩より。平安前期日本と国交の盛んだった
北の国渤海の使節が、芳春の宮中の庭で、音楽に
合わせ現在のポロに似た騎乗球技を披露してみせ
たらしい。それを詠んだ珍しい詩。球を打つ杖が
三日月のようだとあるのは、形が湾曲しているの
を三日月に見立てたのである。嵯峨帝は大陸文明
の摂取に積極的で、弘法大師空海とも親交があっ
た。書に秀いで、空海、橘 逸勢と共に三筆の一
人とされる。

The curved stick might be

a crescent moon flying across the sky

The rushing ball resembles

a comet tumbling to earth

Saga Tennō

Keikokushū, Book XI. From a poem in Chinese entitled "Watching *dakyū* in early spring." It seems that
in the early Heian period envoys from the Chinese
state of Bo Hai, with which Japan then had thriving
relations, used the fragrant spring gardens of the
Imperial palace to show their hosts *dakyū*, a ball game
rather like polo, played on horseback to the accom-
paniment of music. This unusual poem describes
such a scene. The comparison of the stick that drives
the ball to a crescent moon came from the stick's
curved shape. Emperor Saga was an enthusiastic
advocate of continental culture and good friends with
Kūkai (Kōbō Daishi), founder of the Shingon sect of
Buddhism. Famed as well for his calligraphy, he is
considered, with Kūkai and Tachibana no Hayanari,
to be one of the three great masters of that art.

後世は猶
Gose   wa nao

今生だにも
konjō   dani   mo

願はざる
negawazaru

わがふところに
waga   futokoro   ni

さくら来てちる
sakura   kite   chiru

山川登美子
Yamakawa Tomiko

『山川登美子全集』上巻（昭四七）所収。「明星」明治四十一年五月号の「日蔭草」十四首中の一首で、生前発表された最後の歌。結核のため二十九歳で夭折した歌人は、死の一年前すでにこのような自己埋葬の歌を詠んだ。後世はもとより今生にさえ望みを絶ったと覚悟した人のふところに、なお散りかかる桜の幻。これほどに悲劇的な感情が結晶した美しい歌は、古来ごくまれだったと思われる。

Emptied of prayers

for the life to come

or even for this one

my heart is filled

with the falling cherry blossoms

Yamakawa Tomiko

From *Yamakawa Tomiko Zenshū*, Vol. 1, 1972. One of 14 tanka titled "Hikagegusa" (Evergreen Vine), which appeared in the May, 1908 issue of *Myōjō* (Morning Star). These were the last poems Tomiko published in her lifetime, a year before her death from tuberculosis at the age of 29. In them she was already imagining her own body dead and buried. In the heart of one resigned not only to the end of hope for the next life but even for this one, phantom cherry blossoms still scatter. Among the many tanka on cherry blossoms from ancient times, such a beautiful crystallization of a tragic emotion must be very rare.

すかんぽの
Sukanpo   no

茎の味こそ
kuki no aji koso

忘られね
wasurarene

いとけなき日の
itokenaki   hi no

ものの悲しみ
mono   no   kanashimi

吉井　勇
Yoshii Isamu

『酒ほがひ』(明四三)所収。歌についてよく「口当たり」がよいとか悪いとかいう。口当たりがよいというので褒めているのかとおもえば、そうでもない。実は軽薄と言いたいのを粉飾しているにすぎない場合もある。しかし、近代短歌草創期のすぐれた歌人たちの作は、総じて口当たりがよかった。この問題は、今日でも考えるに値するだろう。寛、晶子、牧水、夕暮、啄木、白秋。中でもこの勇。口当たりがよすぎる感はあるが、歌の勘どころは押さえている。

It's the taste

of sorrel stalks

that I can't forget

The sadness of things

when I was young

Yoshii Isamu

From *Sake Hogai* (In Praise of Saké, 1910). Tanka are often talked about in terms of how they "go down," whether their *kuchi atari*, their feel on the palate, is "good" or "bad." "Going down easily" is, contrary to what one might expect, not always a term of praise. Sometimes it is no more than a way of indirectly saying a poem is superficial. However, as a rule, the works of the best poets in the early period of the modern tanka "go down" easily. The problem bears thinking about even today. We have Hiroshi, Akiko, Bokusui, Yūgure, Takuboku, Hakushū. And this Isamu. The poem here goes down almost too easily, but he holds back at the right point.

雲をよび
Kumo wo yobi

乗りて空駆け
norite sora kake

語り合い
katariai

こねてまるめて
konete marumete

食べてしまわん
tabete shimawan

曾宮一念
Somiya Ichinen

『雲をよぶ』(平七)所収。上記は一九九四年末百一歳で没した作者の、没後まもなく編まれた短歌と詩の一冊本選集。縁あって私が編んだ。作者は自作短歌を、本格派でないという意味で「へなぶり」と自称していた。七十八歳で完全失明、画家を廃業後何年もしてから始めたのが短歌だが、晩年十数年間、全くの闇の世界で作られた、驚くべき鮮明な記憶、機智、諷刺、優しさの小宇宙。雲に乗っている、百歳の少年。

I'll call a cloud   climb

on   gallop over the sky

have a good heart-to-heart

then knead it   roll it up

and gobble it downdowndown

Somiya Ichinen

From *Kumo wo yobu* (Calling the Clouds, 1995). This is a collection of the tanka and free verse compiled shortly after the author's death at the age of 101 in 1994. I happened to be the editor. The author termed his own tanka "frivolous," in the sense of not being properly staid. He started to write tanka some years after he went blind and had to give up his career as a painter at the age of 78. During the last fifteen years or so of his life, he created, within a world of total darkness, a microcosm of incredibly clear memories, and of wit, satire and gentleness. A lad of a hundred, riding on a cloud.

端渓の
Tankei no

細かき石の
komakaki ishi no

肌に触れて
hada ni furete

匂ひをあぐる
nioi wo aguru

春の夜の墨
haru no yo no sumi

尾上柴舟
Onoe Saishū

『晴川』(昭二六)所収。柴舟は明治三十年代に金子薫園と「叙景詩」運動を起こして「明星」派に対抗、また明治末「短歌滅亡私論」を書いて話題になったが、自作はむしろ古典的な流麗さで一貫していた。草仮名の名手として著名で、芸術院会員にもなった人であり、博士論文も「平安朝仮名の研究」(大一二)。秀でた仮名の書家だった。ここの「端渓」はもちろん最良の硯石。花のほかにもあった、春夜の香り。

The inkstick is touch-

ing the skin of the stone, which

is from Duan-shi and

fine-grained; now fragrance flows forth,

rises into the spring night. . . .

Onoe Saishū

From *Seisen*, 1951. Saishū, with Kaneko Kunen, began the "descriptive poetry" movement in the third decade of the Meiji period, in opposition to the poets associated with *Myōjō*. And at the end of the Meiji period, he wrote the controversial essay "The Tanka's Demise: A Personal Opinion." His own style, though, always had a classical fluidity. In recognition of his renown as a calligrapher, he was made a member of the Japan Academy of Art; his doctoral thesis, presented in 1923, was *Studies in Kana Calligraphy at the Heian Court*. His *kana* calligraphy was superb. Duan-shi is an area of China where the best inkstones come from. Spring nights are not scented by cherry blossoms alone.

頭の中で
Atama no naka de

白い夏野と
shiroi natsuno to

なつてゐる
natte iru

高屋窓秋
Takaya Sōshū

『白い夏野』(昭十一)所収。「頭」は五七五に則し
て詠めばヅとなる所で、そう読む説もあったが、
作者自身はアタマとしてこれを詠んだという。句
の中心は「白い夏野」の影像にあるから、初五を
ヅという音読みで重くすることはありえなかっ
た。昭和七年、秋桜子の愛弟子だった作者が作っ
たこの句は、俳句革新をこころざす若き俳人たち
に、客観写生・花鳥諷詠とは違う行き方の可能性
を開いたとされ、窓秋初期の代表作として喧伝さ
れた歴史的な意味をもつ句。

The inside of my head

has become

a white summer field

Takaya Sōshū

From *Shiroi Natsuno* (White Summer Field, 1936). The first character would be read as *zu* if the 5-7-5 structure of haiku were observed, and some critics do so; but the author himself has said that he reads it as *atama*. The poem's center is the image "white summer field," so giving weight to the first character by using the Chinese reading *zu* would not work well. Sōshū was a favorite disciple of Mizuhara Shūōshi. In 1932, when he composed this poem, it opened new possibilities for the young haiku poets who were trying to reconstruct the haiku by departing from objective realism and scenes from nature. In this sense, the poem has historical significance; it was widely discussed as one of Sōshū's most important early works.

闘鶏の
Tōkei   no

眼つむれて
manako   tsumurete

飼はれけり
kawarekeri

村上鬼城
Murakami Kijō

『鬼城句集』(大十五) 所収。三百五十石取りの武
家に生まれたが耳を病み、多年高崎裁判所の代書
人として、十人の子持ちの貧しい生活を送った。
年少の正岡子規、ついで高浜虚子に師事。生涯を
見すえて、終始わが道を往く作風だった。目をつ
ぶされた闘鶏はもう使いものにならない。殺され
る所だが飼主の情けで今も飼われている。自らに
ひき較べての切々の情があっても、それは言わず
に鶏だけを描く。

A fighting cock

eyes gone, still kept

still fed

Murakami Kijō

From *Kijō Kushū* (Kijō's Haiku, 1926). Born into a samurai family with an annual income of 350 *koku*, he contracted ear disease and for many years worked as a poorly paid scribe at the Takasaki District Court in order to support his wife and ten children. He studied haiku with the young Masaoka Shiki and then with Takahama Kyoshi. In his style, Kijō confronted life head on and showed a rugged individuality. A blinded fighting cock is of no use anymore. One would expect it to be killed, but out of pity, its owner still keeps it. The poet sees himself in the rooster but avoids sentimentality by letting only the rooster into the poem.

鉦鳴らし
Kane narashi

信濃の国を
Shinano no kuni wo

行き行かば
yuki yukaba

ありしながらの
arishi nagara no

母見るらむか
haha miruramu ka

窪田空穂
Kubota Utsubo

『まひる野』(明三八)所収。信州松本在で生まれた空穂は、母親が四十を過ぎてからの末っ子で、両親に特に愛されて育ったが、青年期に母を、続いて父を喪った。「鉦鳴らし」は巡礼となっての意。「母見るらむか」は母が見るだろうかとも解せるが、作者自身は母を見うるだろうかの意で作ったらしい。「鉦を鳴らし」「母を見る」の「を」が省かれた形だろう。母恋いの歌として愛誦され、牧水の「幾山河越えさりゆかば」の歌にも影響したらしいという。

As I go about

the land of Shinano

ringing my pilgrim's bell,

will I see, perhaps,

my mother as she was then?

Kubota Utsubo

From *Mahiru No* (The Field at High Noon, 1905). Born in the outskirts of Matsumoto in the Shinshū district, Utsubo was the last child, born when his mother was past 40, and especially loved by his parents; but he lost his mother, and then his father, while still a boy. *Kane narashi*, literally "ringing a bell," means he has become a pilgrim. *Haha mirura-mu ka* can be interpreted as "will my mother perhaps see me?" but the author seems to have meant "will I be able to see my mother?" He has, that is, abbreviated the "*wo*" between *haha* and *miruramu*, and also between *kane* and *narashi*. This has been one of the most popular poems about filial love, and may even have influenced the well-known tanka by Wakayama Bokusui that begins, "How many mountains and rivers must I cross . . ."

水鳥の
Mizutori   no

鴨の羽色の
kamo no   hairo   no

春山の
haruyama no

おほつかなくも
ohotsukanaku   mo

思ほゆるかも
omohoyuru   kamo

笠　女郎
Kasa no Iratsume

　『万葉集』巻八春の相聞。作者が大伴家持に贈った恋歌は、たくさんある万葉恋歌の中でも一頭地を抜く観があるものだが、これもその一つ。「水鳥の……春山の」は「おほ（おぼ）つかな」にかかる序詞。春の山が鴨の羽根の色のように深緑の色になっているが、そこに春霞がかかっているため色が全体にぼんやり薄れて見える、そのようにあなたの気持ちもはっきりせず、切ないほど頼りないというのである。比喩の新鮮さが無類。

Among water birds

the wild ducks have wings

the color of spring hills . . .

misted over, now here

now gone, is how I think of you

Kasa no Iratsume

From *Man'yōshū*, Book VIII, Spring Love. There
are many love poems in the *Man'yōshū*, but some
think that those Kasa no Iratsume wrote to Ōtomo
no Yakamochi, of which this is one, are the best of
all. From *mizutori no* to *haruyama no* ("Among
water birds . . . spring hills") is a *joshi* or introducto-
ry phrase for *ohotsukana* (the modern *obotsukana*).
The spring hills are the deep green of the wild
ducks' feathers, but because of the spring mists their
color can only be seen dimly. Your feelings are just
as unclear, she says, and in my misery I do not know
where to turn. A wonderfully fresh metaphor.

逝く水の
Yuku mizu no

流れの底の
nagare no soko no

美しき
utsukushiki

小石に似たる
koishi ni nitaru

思ひ出もあり
omoide mo ari

湯川秀樹
Yukawa Hideki

『深山木』(私家本・昭四六、のち『湯川秀樹著作集』7)所収。澄んだ川水のしんとした流れを見つめている時、人は多かれ少なかれ瞑想家になる。孔子は川のほとりに立って、「逝く者はかくのごときか、昼夜をおかず」と呟いた。川水は生と死の両岸を洗う。作者が少年時代を思い起こしつつ、「逝く」水の流れを思ったのは興味深い。この中間子の予言者は、老荘思想や和歌に親しむ人でもあった。専門外の著作で自ら繰返しのべている通りである。

There are memories

which resemble

the beautiful pebbles

beneath the flow

of passing water

Yukawa Hideki

From *Miyamagi* (Deep Mountain Trees), privately published 1971, later in *Yukawa Hideki Chosakushū*, Vol. 7. Gazing at the silent flow of clear river water often brings on a meditative mood. Confucius, standing by a river bank, whispered, "Is the passing of time like this? Always flowing on . . ." The river's water washes up against the twin shores of life and death. It does not seem completely coincidental that as he was remembering his own youth, the author thought of the flow of "passing water," with its echo of Confucius. This Nobel Prize-winner in physics, who predicted the discovery of the meson, was also a longtime student of the ancient Chinese philosophers Lao-tze and Chuang-tze and of traditional Japanese poetry. His repeated discussions of those subjects in his popular works attest to his knowledge.

目には青葉
Me ni wa aoba

山時鳥
yama hototogisu

初鰹
hatsugatsuo

山口素堂
Yamaguchi Sodō

　作者名は関係なしに多くの人に愛誦されている句の代表格だろう。素堂は芭蕉と親交のあった江戸の俳人。諸芸に通じていた人という。句は「鎌倉にて」の前書がある。目のためには青葉、耳のためにはほととぎす、初夏の最もさわやかな景物が鎌倉にはある。それさえあるに、舌のためには鎌倉名物の初鰹までも加わって、何と気持のいい土地か、という。初物好きの江戸人は、初鰹を大いに好んだ。

For eyes, green leaves

Then the mountain cuckoo

and the first bonito

Yamaguchi Sodō

A good example of a poem everyone likes without knowing or caring who wrote it. Sodō was an Edo haiku poet who was a close friend of Bashō. He is said to have been well-versed in many arts. The prefatory note to this poem is "In Kamakura." For the eyes, there are green leaves and for the ears, the cuckoo's song: Kamakura has the freshest seasonal things of early summer. On top of that, for the tongue you have as well the first bonito, one of Kamakura's famous products. What a refreshing place it is, he says. Edoites, who liked the first things of all seasons, took special delight in the first bonito.

菜の花や
Na no hana ya

月は東に
tsuki wa higashi ni

日は西に
hi wa nishi ni

蕪村
Buson

山もと遠く
Yamamoto tōku

鷺かすみ行
sagi kasumi yuku

樗良
Chora

『続明烏』(蕪村・几董・樗良三吟歌仙)所収。蕪村の句は単独でもきわめて有名だが、樗良とのこの付け合いも有名で、十八世紀後半ののどかな田園風景が一望のもとに見渡せるような気分にさせてくれる。蕪村の句は人麻呂の「東の野にかぎろひの」の歌を連想させ、樗良の句は有名な「水無瀬三吟」の宗祇の発句、「雪ながら山もと霞む夕かな」を借りたものか。その点でも雰囲気は悠然たるもの。

Mustard flowers . . .

the moon in the east

the sun in the west

Buson

Far off at the mountain's foot

herons fade into the mist

Chora

From *Zoku akegarasu*, a linked verse sequence by Buson, Kitō and Chora. Buson's verse has long been celebrated and Chora's reply to it is well known too. Read together, it is as if one's eyes were sweeping over a pastoral landscape of the late 18th century in panoramic fashion. Buson's verse recalls Hitomaro's tanka that begins, "In the eastern fields/the light of dawn (*hingashi no/no ni kagiroi no*). Chora's may have been inspired by Sōgi's opening verse for the famous linked verse sequence *Minase Sangin Hyakuin* (Three Poets at Minase), "Snow there is and yet . . ./mist wraps the mountain foot/this evening" (*yuki nagara/yamamoto kasumu/yūbe kana*). These allusions to poets centuries earlier also contribute to the sense of immensity.

花は根に
Hana wa ne ni

鳥は古巣に
tori wa furusu ni

帰るなり
kaeru nari

春のとまりを
Haru no tomari wo

知る人ぞなき
shiru hito zo naki

崇徳院
Sutoku In

『千載集』巻二春下。歴代天皇の中でも崇徳院ほ
どに悲運だった帝王も少なかろう。出生自体にす
でに暗い影があり、そのため父鳥羽天皇にうとん
じられたという。保元の乱の主役となり、最後は
讃岐に配流、そこで崩じた。しかし崇徳院は歴代
天皇の中でも抜きんでた歌人の一人で、心情のよ
く流露する歌を作った人。この歌は晩春を詠む。
花は散って根に帰り、鳥は古巣に戻るが、ひとり
春だけはどこに宿るのか、帰りゆく先を知る者も
ない。

The flowers have gone back

to their roots, the birds

to their old nests

Who knows where spring

is gone to rest?

Sutoku In

Senzaishū, Book II, Spring 1. Very few Japanese emperors have had as tragic a life as Sutoku. A shadow was cast even over the circumstances of his birth, and it is said that that was why his father, Emperor Toba, shunned him. He played a leading role in the Hōgen War, and as a result was exiled to the island of Sanuki, where he died. But Sutoku was also one of the very best poets among all the emperors, and his poems express emotion eloquently. This poem is about late spring. The flowers have scattered and returned to their roots, and the birds have returned to their old nests; only spring is untraceable—no one knows where it is staying now, or to where it has returned.

月の輝くは
Tsuki no kagayaku wa

晴れたる雪の如し
haretaru yuki no gotoshi

梅花は
Baika wa

照れる星に似たり
tereru hoshi ni nitari

菅原道真
Sugawara no Michizane

　道真詩集『菅原文草』巻頭の「月夜梅花を見る」の起承部。同集は制作年代順の構成でこの詩は十一歳当時の処女作。続く転結部では、心動かされることだ、金鏡（月）がくるめく庭に、梅の玉なす房がふくいくと香っている、と詠む。少年道真の詩作の師は、父の是善やその門人島田忠臣だったと思われる。今の年齢だと十歳だろう。ういういしいが印象鮮明、後年の大才ぶりが早くも示されている。

The moon sparkles like

new fallen snow

The plum blossoms resemble

shining stars

Sugawara no Michizane

The first two lines of "A View of Plum Blossoms on a Spring Night," the first poem in Michizane's collection of Chinese poetry, *Kanke Bunshō*. The collection is ordered by year of composition, so this is Michizane's first poem, written when he was 11 (or, by modern count, 10). The third and fourth lines read (in paraphrase) "How lovely! In the garden where the golden mirror (the moon) sheds its light, pearl-like clusters of plum blossoms give off scent." It is thought that the young Michizane's tutors in poetry were his father Koreyoshi and his father's disciple Shimada Tadaomi. This poem, artless as it is, gives an impression of freshness and is early evidence of Michizane's great talent.

さくらばな
Sakurabana

花体を解きて
katai   wo   tokite

人のふむ
hito   no   fumu

こまかき砂利に
komakaki   jari   ni

交りけるかも
majirikeru   kamo

岡本かの子
Okamoto Kanoko

『深見草』(昭十五)所収。かの子は昭和四年四十
歳で『わが最終歌集』を出した。小説家になりた
い一心だった。しかし小説家の才能がまさに爆発
的に開花したのは、四十七歳の時の作『鶴は病み
き』が最初で、二年余り後には脳出血で倒れる。
没後続々と傑作が発表され、世間を驚倒させた。
同じく歌集『深見草』も没後の刊行。作風は上の
歌のように、微細なものへの注視に特徴があり、
悠然として閑静。

Cherry blossoms

having shed their flower-bodies

are folded in

among the fine gravel

where people walk

Okamoto Kanoko

From *Fukamigusa* (Peonies, 1940). Determined to devote herself to fiction, Kanoko published her last tanka collection, *Waga Saishū Kashū*, in 1929, when she was 40 years old. But the first explosive flowering of her talent as a writer of fiction was only at the age of 47, with *Tsuru wa Yamiki* (The Crane Sickened). She died only a few years later, of a cerebral hemorrhage. Then came, to the astonishment of the general public, a succession of posthumous masterpieces, of which *Fukamigusa* was one. Kanoko's style, as the poem above shows, is marked by its focus on fine detail and a balanced tranquility.

あけぼのの
Akebono   *no*

春あけぼのの
haru   *akebono*   *no*

水の音
mizu   *no*   *oto*

野沢節子
Nozawa Setsuko

『駿河蘭』(平八)所収。平成七年四月九日、七十五歳で没した代表的女性俳人の一人。遺句集だが、上の句には「蘇生」と題があり、病状深刻な時の、ある明け方の句とわかる。これに並ぶ句に「春 曙夢中の滝を見つづけて」。後日の句にも、「さみだれを咳つつ夢に旅しをり」など、夢をしばしば句にしているのは、まさに俳人魂。「絶句」は「牡丹雪しばらく息をつがぬまま」。痛ましくも壮絶な句である。

In daybreak is the

spring, in daybreak is the

water's sound

Nozawa Setsuko

From *Suruga ran*, 1996. A leading female haiku poet, who died on April 9, 1995, at the age of 75. The collection was posthumous, but the haiku is titled "Return to life"; evidently it was written one dawn when her condition was very grave. Along with it is this poem: "Spring dawn . . . looking and/ looking at a waterfall/in a dream" (*haru akebono/ muchū no taki wo / mitsuzukete*). Like a true haiku poet, she continued to make her dreams into poems, as in the later "Coughing in the summer/rain as I travel/in a dream" (*samidare wo / sekitsutsu yume ni / tabi shi ori*). On her deathbed, she wrote: "Peony-like snow . . ./for a little while my breath/is lost" (*botan yuki / shibaraku iki wo / tsuganu mama*). A poem pitiful and yet sublime.

春の日に
Haru no hi ni

萌れる柳を
hareru yanagi wo

取り持ちて
tori mochite

見れば都の
mireba miyako no

大路し思ほゆ
ōji shi omohoyu

大伴家持
Ōtomo no Yakamochi

『万葉集』巻十九。大伴家持はこれを作った天平勝宝二年三月二日現在、越中守（いわば富山県知事）として、すでに四年半が過ぎていた。任期は六年というのが普通の例だったようだが、彼は越中では詩人としても充実した暮らしを楽しむ反面、さすがに望郷の念もしきりだったようだ。春の一日、うら若い芽ぶき柳を見て、奈良の大路の柳の街路樹をそこに夢みている、都会っ子貴公子の面影。

On a spring day I take

a budding willow in my hand

and the sight of it

brings back

the capital's boulevards

Ōtomo no Yakamochi

From *Man'yōshū*, Book XIX. When he wrote this poem on the second day of the third lunar month of the year 750 A.D., Ōtomo no Yakamochi had already spent four and a half years as the governor of Etchū (now Toyama Prefecture). Six years was considered the usual term of office, but while enjoying his life as a poet in Etchū, it seems that Yakamochi never lost his homesickness for Nara, the capital. One spring day, looking at the young and budding willow trees, he fell to dreaming of the rows of willow trees that lined its boulevards. A portrait of a young, urban aristocrat.

水に浮く
Mizu ni uku

柄杓の上の
hishaku no ue no

春の雪
haru no yuki

高浜虚子
Takahama Kyoshi

『五百句』(昭十二)所収。虚子の句には、小さな事物を通して大きな世界を一気に暗示する句が多い。「ものの芽のあらはれ出でし大事かな」と吟じている通りである。「蝶々のもの食ふ音の静かさよ」「桐一葉日当りながら落ちにけり」「蛇逃げて我を見し眼の草に残る」。上の句も同じ。浮く柄杓がすでに軽い。その上にふわりと積もった春雪はさらに軽い。そして句が暗示するのは、春そのもの。

Spring snow

covers a ladle

floating on water

Takahama Kyoshi

From *Gohyakku*, (500 Haiku, 1937). Kyoshi's haiku often offer a sudden glimpse of large worlds through a concentration on small things. There is, for example, his "So much depends/on the coming into bud/ of things" (*mono no me no/araware ideshi/daiji kana*). And also: "How quiet/is the sound/of a butterfly eating" (*chōchō no/mono kuu oto no/shizukasa yo*); "A single paulownia leaf,/bathed in sunlight,/fell" (*kiri hitoha/hi atarinagara/ochinikeri*); "The snake fled,/its eyes that saw me/left behind in the grass" (*hebi nigete/ware wo mishi me no/kusa ni nokoru*). The haiku above is of this sort, too. A floating ladle is light to begin with, the soft spring snow piled on top of it lighter still. And what the poem suggests is all of spring itself.

たくあんの
Takuan   no

波利と音して
hari   to   oto   shite

梅ひらく
ume   hiraku

加藤楸邨
Katō Shūson

　『吹越』（昭五一）所収。「波利」はハリと読むのか
それともパリか。後者の方が実際の音には近いが、
この場合にはあえてハリと読むべきだろう。たぶ
ん作者は、「波利」と意識的に漢字で書いて、パ
リという音をうしろに漂わせながら、ハリの音に
軽やかに遊んでいるのである。その結果「梅ひら
く」がこの音と優しく響き合う。たくあんと梅の
花がこんな形で結びつけられるのを見ることに、
詩を読むだいご味もあるといえる。

The crunch of

pickled radish—

plum blossoms open

Katō Shūson

From *Fukkoshi*, 1967. Should the characters 波利 be read *hari* or *pari*? *Pari* is closer to the true sound the radish makes when someone bites into it, but even so I think the characters should be read as *hari*. The poet has deliberately written the word with kanji, which leaves room for both readings, as if he were lightly juggling the two possibilities. Thus the *hira* of *ume hiraku* echoes softly against *pari / hari*, the pickly crunch. Being able to see pickles and plum blossoms linked in this unexpected way gives a taste of the pleasures of poetry.

夏のうた

SUMMER POEMS

牡丹散て
Botan   chirite

打かさなりぬ
uchi-kasanarinu

二三片
ni   san   pen

与謝蕪村
Yosa Buson

『蕪村句集』所収。「散て」は、句から受ける印象からするとチッテと読みたいところだが、蕪村自身はある手紙の中で「ちりて」と書いている。だがチッテも捨て難い。中国では花の王とまで称えられる大輪の牡丹は、日本でも江戸前期から盛んに栽培鑑賞された。この句、散り敷いた花びらを「打ちかさなりぬ二三片」と詠みすえた所が手練のわざ。散った花のいさぎよさ、反面の濃艶な色香、その両面をひたと取り押さえているからだ。

Peony petals fall,

pile up—

two or three

Yosa Buson

From *Buson Kushū*. The effect of the poem as a whole makes one want to read the third character as *chitte*, but Buson himself wrote it out in a letter as *chirite*. Even so, *chitte* has its own attractions. The Chinese called the peony, with its large blossoms, the emperor of flowers; and from the 17th century on, the Japanese cultivated it devotedly as an ornamental flower. The firmness with which he writes *uchikasanarinu / nisanpen* (pile up— / two or three) is the mark of craft. It captures perfectly both aspects of the fallen petals—their heroic purity and their sensual charm.

卯の花に
U　no　hana　ni

蘆毛の馬の
ashige　no　uma　no

夜明哉
yoake　kana

森川許六
Morikawa Kyoriku

『炭俵』所収。「旅行に」と題する。許六は芭蕉
最晩年の弟子で多才な論客だった。三百石の彦根
藩士で、これは元禄六年五月はじめ江戸をたち彦
根に帰った時の作らしい。「蘆毛」は白い毛に黒
や濃褐色のさし毛のある馬で、道ぞいに咲く卯の
花の鮮やかな白との色の取り合わせが眼目。しか
も夜明けだ。初夏の気分が溢れている。そういえ
ば、夜明けに馬ではなく、自動車で旅立つような
現代の日常の情景を爽やかに詠んだ現代の句はま
だ知らない。

Deutzia flowers

and a dappled horse

at dawn

Morikawa Kyoriku

From *Sumidawara* (Charcoal Sack). Titled "On a trip." Kyoriku, a disciple of Basho's last years, was a samurai of the 300-*koku* fief of Hikone and a man of many talents. This poem seems to have been written on his way back to Hikone from Edo in early May, 1693. The poem's center is the juxtaposition of the horse's black and brown speckled whiteness with the fresh white of the flowers by the side of the road. The time is dawn, and the mood of early summer permeates the scene. This reminds me: I have yet to encounter a contemporary haiku which treats the everyday event of setting off on a trip at dawn—not by horse, of course, but by car— in this refreshing way.

青海原
Ao-unabara

藻の花ゆらぐ
mo no hana yuragu

波の底に
nami no soko ni

魚とし住まば
uo to shi sumaba

悶えざらむか
modaezaramu ka

芥川龍之介
Akutagawa Ryūnosuke

　　書簡集より。明治四十二年、府立三中最後の年
の春、千葉県銚子に遊んだ時、親友西村貞吉に送
った絵葉書にしるした歌。芥川の短歌では最も初
期に属する作である。海底で魚と一緒に住んだな
ら、悶えることもなくてすむだろうか、と。少年
の感傷と言ってしまえばそれまでだが、「悶えざ
らむか」には、憂鬱のしぼり出すような力がある。
芥川は大正五年ごろまで、一高以来の親友恒藤恭
ら何人もの友人にしばしば短歌を書き送ってい
る。

If I lived with the fishes

in the deep blue ocean, sea

flowers swaying beneath

the waves, would this

pain, this anguish be eased?

Akutagawa Ryūnosuke

From Akutagawa's collected letters. Akutagawa wrote this tanka, one of his earliest works, on a picture postcard he sent to his close friend Nishimura Teikichi while vacationing at Chōshi, Chiba Prefecture. It was the spring of 1909 and he was 17. It is easy to dismiss this poem as an expression of youthful sentimentality, but *modaezaramu ka* ("would this/pain, this anguish be eased?") has a concentrated power, as though his melancholy had forcibly squeezed it out. Akutagawa continued to send tanka to Tsunetō Kyō and other close friends until 1916.

月は船
Tsuki wa fune

星は白波
hoshi wa shiranami

雲は海
kumo wa umi

いかに漕ぐらん
Ika ni koguran

桂男は
katsura-otoko wa

ただ一人して
tada hitori shite

梁塵秘抄
Ryōjin Hishō

『万葉集』巻七冒頭に柿本人麻呂歌集からとして
ある一首、「天の海に雲の波立ち月の船星の林に
漕ぎ隠る見ゆ」と、内容といい発想といい、大層
よく似ている。『梁塵秘抄』は平安末期に後白河
院が編ませた平安歌謡集だが、その中の一首と古
代の人麻呂歌集との類似は偶然とも思えない。少
なくとも夜空を見てそこに大海原を想定するとい
う想像力の一つの型があったのであろう。違いは
後代の歌には月に住むという「桂男」の孤影が現
れること。

The moon a boat

the stars white waves

the clouds an ocean

And the laurel man

rows all alone—

how will he ever make his way?

Ryōjin Hishō

This poem very closely resembles in conception the first one of *Man'yōshū* Book VII, said to be from the Hitomaro Collection: "In the sea of heaven/cloud waves rise/and the moon boat sails/into a forest of stars,/to be seen no more" (*ame no umi ni / kumo no nami tachi / tsuki no fune / hoshi no hayashi ni / kogika-kuru miyu*). The *Ryōjin Hishō*, a collection of folk songs from the 11th century on, was compiled late in the Heian period under the direction of retired Emperor Goshirakawa, but the resemblance between one of its poems and the ancient Hitomaro Collection can hardly have been coincidental. At the very least, there must have been an imaginative tradition that metamorphosed the night sky into an ocean. The only difference is the appearance in the later poem of a solitary figure, "the laurel man" (*katsura-otoko*), that is, the man in the moon.

垢なりや塵なりや
Aka nari ya Chiri nari ya

是れ何物なりや
Kore nani mono nari ya

元来見来れば
Ganrai mi kitareba

更に無骨なり
sara ni bukotsu nari

一休宗純
Ikkyū Sōjun

『江戸漢詩集』所収。室町時代の傑僧一休は、ま
た卓越した漢詩・狂詩の作者だった。これは『一
休諸国物語』中の狂詩で、「蚤に題す」とある七
言絶句の起・承二句。おいこれは垢か、塵か、一
体何だ。見れば骨もない不細工なやつめ。この二
句に続く転・結二句は「人を喰ひて十分に肥えた
りといへども、痩僧の一ひねりにも生涯を没せ
ん」。ノミに寄せて、世の不徳義漢どもの空しい
権勢富貴を一喝したか。

What's this

   —Old skin? Dust?

A close look tells all

   —boneless freaks.

Ikkyū Sōjun

From *Edo Kanshi Shū*. Ikkyū, that great priest of the Muromachi period, also wrote wonderful Chinese poetry, both serious and "wild," that is, satirical. These are the first two lines of a four-line "wild" poem from "Tales of Ikkyū's Travels." It is titled "On Fleas," and the last two lines go: "They've grown fat on human flesh/but this thin priest can do them in with a single pinch." (*hito wo kuraite jūbun ni koetari to iedomo / sōsō no hitohineri ni mo shōgai wo bossen*) Was the flea a means to protest the immoral power and vain glory he saw around him?

うすものの
Usumono *no*

二尺のたもと
nishaku *no* *tamoto*

すべりおちて
suberi *ochite*

蛍ながるる
hotaru *nagaruru*

夜風の青き
yokaze *no* *aoki*

与謝野晶子
Yosano Akiko

『みだれ髪』(明三四)所収。晶子は歌に数詞を読みこむのを好んだし巧みでもあった。「髪五尺」「三尺の船」「千すぢの髪」「はたち妻」その他。数詞は内容に明確な輪郭を与える点で大いに有効な場合があるが、それも使い手の力量による。うすものの衣の長いたもとを、光るしずくのようにほろほろ滑り、飛び去る蛍。夜風も青いさわやかな宵の讃歌。今ではそれも失われた幻に近いが。

Down silken sleeve

two feet long

fireflies glide and slide,

then flow

into the evening breeze's green

Yosano Akiko

From *Midaregami* (Tangled Hair, 1901). Akiko liked to weave numbers into her poems and did it well: "hair five feet long," "a three-foot boat," "a thousand strands of hair," "a twenty-year-old wife," are a few examples. In the hands of a skillful poet, such usage can add clarity to the poem's images. Like shining drops, fireflies slide down the long sleeves of a young girl's thin summer kimono, then fly off. The evening breeze is so fresh it seems green. Now such a scene is close to a dream from a lost world.

一つ蛍
Hitotsu hotaru

ひかり惜しまず
hikari　　　oshimazu

高昇り
takanobori

岸田稚魚
Kishida Chigyo

『紅葉山』（平元）所収。作者は昭和六十三年十一月七十歳で死去した。上記は一周忌に刊行の遺句集。「ゆきどまりまで来しわが世虫のこゑ」「死ぬることの幸ひ銀河流れをり」のような句には、死を前にして到達した境涯詠作者としての稚魚の面目がうかがえる。句集題名ともなった「紅葉山いろんな色に落着かず」も面白い。そういう目で見れば、上の句は作者の祈願をこめた自画像だったか。

A single firefly

begrudging no light

wings high

Kishida Chigyo

From *Momijiyama* (The Autumn Hills, 1989). The author died in November 1988, at the age of 70. The haiku collection published to commemorate the first anniversary of his death, in which the poem above appears, also includes: "At the end of the road,/my life—/the insects' voices" (*yukidomari / made koshi waga yo / mushi no koe*); and "The bliss of dying—/The Milky Way/flows above" (*shinuru koto no/saiwai ginga/nagare ori*). Poems like this are witness to what Chigyo achieved as an autobiographical poet, as he confronted death. The poem from which the collection takes its name is also interesting: "The autumn hills—/restless/in their many colors" (*momijiyama / ironna iro ni / ochitsu-kazu*). After reading such poems, one thinks of the poem above as a self-portrait, and also a prayer.

天の海に
Ame no umi ni

雲の波立ち
kumo no nami tachi

月の船
tsuki no fune

星の林に
hoshi no hayashi ni

漕ぎ隠る見ゆ
kogikakuru miyu

柿本人麻呂集
Kakinomoto no Hitomaro Kashū

『万葉集』巻七雑歌冒頭。広大な天の海。そこに
浮かぶ雲は、立つ白波だ。月の船がそこを渡って、
星の林に隠れてゆく。『万葉集』にはすぐれた叙
景歌が多いが、中での異色作。「星の林」という
見立てかたが面白い。原文の万葉仮名は「天海丹
雲之波立 月船 星之林丹 榜隠所見」。天海を
漕ぎ渡る月船を見ながら、他の星からくるUFOの
ごとき物体を夢みた古代人もいたかもしれない。

In the sea of heaven

cloud waves rise and

the moon boat sails

into a forest of stars,

then is seen no more

Kakinomoto no Hitomaro
Poetry Collection

The first poem of Book VII, Miscellaneous Poems, of the *Man'yōshū*. The vast sea of heaven. And the clouds floating in it are high, foaming waves. The moon, a boat, crosses them, and disappears into a forest of stars. Of the many beautiful descriptive poems in the *Man'yōshū* this is one of the more unusual. I like the metaphor "a forest of stars." Someone in ancient times may have looked at the moon boat crossing the heavenly sea and fantasized something like a UFO come from a far-off star.

常しへに
Tokoshie　ni

君も逢へやも
kimi　mo　aeyamo

いさなとり
isanatori

海の浜藻の
umi　no　hamamo　no

寄る時々を
yoru　tokidoki　wo

日本書紀歌謡
Nihon Shoki　kayō

　容姿のあまりの美しさに、衣を通してまで光っ
たので衣通郎姫の名があるという古代最高の美女
の歌。允恭天皇の皇后の妹で、天皇の寵愛を受け
た。茅淳の宮に住まわせていた郎姫のもとへ天皇
が行幸した時彼女が歌った歌。イサナトリは「海」
の枕詞。海藻が時々浜に寄せる（そのように時を
置いてではなく）、いつもいつも逢ってください、
というのである。風土色が自然に恋の歌に独特な
生気を通わせている。

I want to be with you forever

though the grasses

of the whale-hunting sea

come to shore

but from time to time

Nihon Shoki song

The speaker is the most beautiful woman of the ancient world, Sotōri-no-Iratsume, or Princess Passing-Through-Her-Robes, so named, it is said, because her body was so beautiful it shone through her robes. Emperor Ingyō, who was married to her elder sister, fell in love with her and installed her in the Chinu Palace. She recited this poem when he came to visit her there. *Isanatori*, "whale-hunting," is a pillow-word for *umi*, "sea." I want you to be with me forever, she says, not like the seaweed that comes to the beach, only from time to time. Imagery drawn from the local landscape gave a lively individuality to this love poem.

かなしみを乳房のように
Kanashimi wo chibusa no yō ni

まさぐり
masaguri

かなしみをはなれたら
Kanashimi wo hanaretara

死のうとしてゐる
shinō to shite iru

八木重吉
Yagi Jūkichi

『貧しき信徒』(昭三)所収。詩人八木重吉は二十
九歳で夭折した。生前『秋の瞳』一冊を出したの
みだったが、以後『貧しき信徒』を先頭に遺稿が
続々と刊行され、現在では広く愛読される詩人の
一人である。詩にはこの「かなしみ」という二行
詩のように、ごく短い詩が多いが、盛られている
思想は、逆説と見えてはっとさせるほど真実をつ
いたものがある。この詩にも、裸形にされた人間
の心がある。

I grope for sadness as for the breast

and if I let the sadness go, I will die

Yagi Jūkichi

From *Mazushiki Shinto* (The Poor Believer, 1928).
The poet Yagi Jūkichi died at the age of 29, having
published while alive only one book of poetry, *Aki
no Hitomi* (Autumn Eyes). *Mazushiki Shinto* was the
first of several posthumous books compiled from
the manuscripts he left behind. Today he is a popular
and widely read poet. Many of his poems, like this
two-line one, "Sadness," are very short, but his
thought is rich in seeming paradoxes which suddenly and surprisingly reveal the truth. In this poem,
we have the naked human heart.

妊りて
Migomorite

紅き日傘を
akaki　higasa　wo

小さくさす
chiisaku　sasu

森　澄雄
Mori Sumio

『雪櫟』(昭二九)所収。年譜に照らすと、この句
は昭和二十五年、作者三十一歳当時の作のようだ。
二年前結婚、長男に続いて長女が生まれようとす
る夏の作。終戦直後、生活面では悪戦苦闘の時代
だが、この妻の愛らしい肖像画に溢れているいと
おしさの感情は、家族への愛が厳しい時代を耐え
抜くための強い支えだったことを想像させる。
「雪櫟夜の奈落に妻子ねて」という句が「自序」
である。

Belly baby full

she shades herself small

with a poppy parasol

Mori Sumio

From *Yukitsubute*, 1954. In light of Mori's chronology, this poem was probably written in 1950 when he was 31. Married two years before, his second child, a girl, was on her way that summer; the first had been a boy. It was just after the war's end, when simply getting food and lodging was a struggle in itself, but this charming portrait of his wife overflows with a warmth of feeling that suggests that one of the main supports which helped him survive that terrible time was the love he felt for his family. "Snow blowing like pebbles /In the deep bottom of the night/my wife my children sleep" (*yukitsubute / yoru no naraku ni / saishi nete*) is his epigraph for the whole collection.

かぜ と なりたや
Kaze to naritaya

はつなつの
Hatsunatsu no

かぜ と なりたや
kaze to naritaya

川上澄生
Kawakami Sumio

『川上澄生全集』第一巻（昭和五四）所収。詩人画家澄生の有名な木版画「初夏の風」（大一五）に彫られている自作の詩の冒頭。続けて「かのひとのまへにはだかり　かのひとのうしろよりふく　はつなつのはつなつの　かぜとなりたや」。画面には、ドレスのスカートを吹きあげられて恥じらっている乙女を中央に、緑のいたずらな風が踊るのびやかな風景が描かれている。棟方志功はこの一点を見て版画を志した。

Let me become the breeze!

Let me become

the first breeze of summer!

Kawakami Sumio

From *Kawakami Sumio Zenshū*, Volume I, 1979. Kawakami was a poet and an artist. This is the beginning of a poem he wrote in 1926 and carved into his woodblock print "The First Breeze of Summer." It goes on: "I'd stand in front and block her way / I'd blow from behind / Oh let me be / summer's first, first breeze!" (*kano hito no mae ni hadakari/kano hito no ushiro yori fuku/hatsunatsu no/ kaze to nartaya*). The woodblock shows a fresh and lively scene with an embarrassed young woman at the center, her skirt being blown up by a mischievous green breeze. This was the work that inspired Munakata Shikō to become a wookblock print artist.

ゆふぐれは
Yūgure wa

雲のはたてに
kumo no hatate ni

ものぞ思ふ
mono zo omou

天つ空なる
amatsu sora naru

人をこふとて
hito wo kou tote

よみ人しらず
Yomibito shirazu

『古今集』巻十一恋。「雲のはたてに」は雲のはてに。「天つ空なる人」は天上にいる人、つまり手の届かぬはるかな高みにいる想い人。作者はたぶん男性で、想う相手は、当時の身分制度のもとでは手の届かぬ高嶺の花の女性だったのだろう。しかし一首には、そういう現実の事情をこえて、恋する人に共通のあこがれと悩みが歌われている。この歌は広く愛誦され、空をながめて嘆く片思いの歌の一典型となった。

When evening falls,

my reveries turn

to the farthest clouds,

for I love one who dwells

in the vast skies above

Anonymous

Kokinshū, Book XI, Love. *Kumo no hatate ni* means to the end of the clouds. *Amatsu sora naru hito* means a person in the sky above, that is, a person one loves but who is impossibly far above one in rank. The speaker is probably male, and the object of his affections a woman of such high rank that, under the prevailing social system, he could never win her. The poem, however, transcends such realistic circumstances and expresses the longing and anguish common to all who love. This poem has enjoyed wide popularity, and is the prototype of poems about the melancholy, unrequited lover gazing at the sky.

蛸壺や
Takotsubo   ya

はかなき夢を
Hakanaki   yume wo

夏の月
natsu no tsuki

松尾芭蕉
Matsuo Bashō

　芭蕉は貞享五年の関西への旅で、須磨・明石地方を訪ねた。この時の紀行文『笈の小文』に出る句。「蛸壺」は蛸が穴に隠れる習性を利用した、捕獲用の素焼きの壺。昼のうちに海底に沈め、早朝に引きあげる。夏の短か夜、月が海を照らす。海底の壺の暗がりの中に、短か夜のはかない命の夢を結ぶ生きものがうずくまっている。一読して「あわれ」の感が深い句だが、底には非情な俳諧的「おかし」の達観を秘めている。

Octopus pots!

Fleeting dreams,

the summer moon

Matsuo Bashō

On his trip of 1688 to western Japan, Bashō visited Suma and Akashi. This haiku appears in his travel journal from that time, *Oi no Kobumi* (Backpack Manuscripts). *Takotsubo*, "octopus pots": unpainted ceramic pots which used the propensity of octopuses for hiding in holes as a way to trap them. The fishermen lowered the pots to the bottom of the sea during the day, then pulled them up before dawn. On brief summer nights, the moon lights up the sea. In the darkness of a pot on the sandy floor, a living creature swirls about, dreaming fleeting dreams of a life brief as the night. On first reading, the poem has a deep feeling of pathos, but at its core lies *okashi*, a kind of humorous detachment toward the absurdity of life that is often found in haikai.

ブラウスの
Burausu　　*no*

中まで明るき
naka　*made*　*akaruki*

初夏の陽に
shoka　*no*　*hi*　*ni*

けぶれるごとき
kebureru　　*gotoki*

わが乳房あり
waga　*chibusa*　*ari*

河野裕子
Kawano Yūko

『森のやうに獣のやうに』(昭四七)所収。「女性は自らの特殊性をそうあっさりと捨てさるべきではあるまい」。作者は近年の評論で、『古事記歌謡』の時代は別として女性が乳房をうたった歌が、与謝野晶子の登場するまで、千三百年の間存在しなかったことにふれ、こう書いたことがある。第一歌集にある上の歌、「けぶれるごとき」に、命の安らかな広がりの感覚があり、女である自分に対する健康な自己愛がある。

Even the inside

of my blouse is bright

in the early summer sun

and in that light my breasts

sway softly, dimly glowing

Kawano Yūko

From *Mori no yō ni kemono no yō ni* (Like the Forests, Like the Beasts, 1972). "A woman should not abandon her own particularity so lightly." So said Kawano herself, in a recent critical essay, as a comment on the fact that during the 1300 years between the period of the *Kojiki* and the advent of Yosano Akiko, poems by women that mention breasts did not exist. The poem above is from her first collection of tanka. The phrase *keburēru gotoki*, "sway softly dimly glowing," gives a tranquil, expansive sensation, and conveys a healthy love for herself as a woman.

もの思へば
Mono omoeba

沢の螢も
sawa no hotaru mo

わが身より
wagami yori

あくがれ出づる
akugareizuru

魂かとぞ見る
tama ka to zo miru

和泉式部
Izumi Shikibu

『後拾遺集』雑六。愛人に見捨てられていたころ、鞍馬の貴船神社に参籠して、御手洗川に飛ぶ螢を見て詠んだと前書きする。体と魂は本来別物で、深い嘆きに沈んだりすると魂が遊離すると信じられていた。それが「あくがれ」。嘆きに沈んでいると、夕闇に明滅する螢火も、体からさまよい出たわが魂かと見えると。怖れをもって歌っているが調べの張りと艶はみごとである。明神は「奥山にたぎりて落つる滝つ瀬の玉ちるばかりものな思ひそ」と答えたという。

In the river fireflies

I seem to see my soul,

suffused with sadness,

gone forth in longing

from my body

Izumi Shikibu

Goshūishū, Miscellaneous 6. The prefatory note says that Shikibu composed this poem while watching the fireflies fly over Mitarashi River during a retreat at Kibune Shrine in Kurama, after her lover had forsaken her. It was believed that the body and the soul were originally separate, and that the soul split off at times of great sadness, as here, *akugare*, "in longing." Sunk in grief, even the flickering light of the fireflies in the darkness looks like her own soul strayed from her body. The poem's inspiration may have been fear, but the tone is wonderfully strong, almost voluptuous. The god of the shrine is said to have replied: "Do not grieve so long/that your soul becomes like/the spray flying off from/the foaming rapids/as they cascade through remote mountains." (*okuyama ni/tagirite otsuru/takitsuse no/tama chiru bakari/mono na omohi so*).

夜の海に釣りあげた黒鯛
Yoru no umi ni   tsuriageta   kurodai

その眼に新月がいつまでものこっている
Sono me ni shingetsu ga   itsu made mo   nokotte   iru

田中冬二
Tanaka Fuyuji

　詩集『葡萄の女』(昭四一)所収「新月」全文。
昭和五十五年春八十五歳で逝去した詩人。日本各
地の四季の景物に対する敏感な観察と、よく練ら
れた簡潔平明な表現で多くの愛読者をもってい
た。釣った鯛の眼にいつまでも月が映っているな
ど、本当はありえないことだが、鋭くやせた新月
の映像を思い浮かべると、それがありうる事のよ
うに思われてくる。新月だからいいので、満月な
どではぶちこわし。

Black bream fished up from the night sea:

For a long time the new moon remains in its eyes

Tanaka Fuyuji

From the free verse collection *Budō no Onna* (Woman of Grapes, 1966), the poem "New Moon" in its entirety. Tanaka was a free verse poet who died in 1980 at the age of 85. Many readers were devoted to him because of his precise observation of seasonal sights all over Japan and the refined and elegant simplicity of his diction. In reality, the new moon could never be reflected for hours in the eyes of a bream after it has been caught; but imagining the sharp, thin shape of the new moon, it comes to seem possible. Only with the new moon, though: if it were a full moon, the effect would be ruined.

見えぬもの
Mienu mono

見え深沈と
mie shinchin to

夜半の夏
yowa no natsu

富安風生
Tomiyasu Fūsei

『富安風生全句集　補遺篇』(平二)所収。昭和五
十四年九十三歳で没した風生の九十歳当時の作。
上記句集ではこの句の前に「夜半の夏しいんと更
けて十七音」の句がある。十七音とはすなわち俳
句。最晩年まで充実した句作を続け、老年の艶を
たたえられた俳人だが、その俳人が、夏の夜半の
深沈たる静けさの中で句に思いを凝らしている。
自己集中の果て、見えないものまでありありと見
えてくる醍醐味に浸って。

Things unseen

made visible in deep silence—

midnight in summer

Tomiyasu Fūsei

From *Tomiyasu Fūsei Zenkushū, Hoihen*, 1990. Fūsei died in 1979, at age 93; this haiku was written when he was 90. The haiku before it in the volume mentioned above is: "Midnight in summer/deepens to a hush—/seventeen sounds" (*yowa no natsu/shiin to fukete/jūnana on*). "Seventeen sounds" means, of course, a haiku. Fūsei was active as a poet until his last years, and his haiku were praised for possessing a lustrous sheen unique to old age. In these poems, we see him in deep concentration on a quiet summer night, immersed in an ecstasy in which even unseen things take on clear and vivid shapes.

墓地は焼跡
Bochi wa yakeato

蟬肉片の
semi nikuhen no

ごと樹樹に
goto kigi ni

金子兜太
Kaneko Tōta

『少年』（昭三〇）所収。この有名な作品を前にして思うのは、戦後俳句の作品面での全盛期が意外に短かったということである。この句は句集では早くも昭和二十二—三年の「結婚前後」の章に出る。第二芸術論の衝撃に俳句界が激震状態となり、それに反発して、こういう野性味ある革新的な句も作られたのだった。いわば強音を連打する作句法で、一時期はそれも有効だったが、その波も知らぬ間に、意外に早く引いていった。そこに戦後があった。

The graveyard a bombed ruin:

Like bits of flesh, cicadas

on the trees

Kaneko Tōta

From *Shōnen* (Young Boy, 1955). Looking at this famous work now, what strikes me is how short the post-war haiku renaissance really was in terms of the poems themselves. This haiku appears in the chapter "Around the time of my marriage," that is 1947–48. At the time, the haiku world was in a state of turmoil because of the attack on haiku as a second class art, and works like this—innovative and almost feral—were one response. It is constructed as a series of fortissimo images, a technique which was effective for a while, but then passed its peak at some point and disappeared almost before one knew it. Such was the rhythm of the post-war years.

桃二つ
Momo futatsu

寄りて泉に
yorite   izumi ni

打たるるを
utaruru   wo

かすかに夜の
kasuka   ni yoru no

闇に見ている
yami ni   mite   iru

高安国世
Takayasu Kuniyo

『街上』(昭三七)所収。読んでゆくうち、泉に打
たれている桃を、読者自身、闇を透かして見つめ
るような気分にさせられる歌。腐蝕銅版画的効果
とでもいえようか。作者はリルケの翻訳者として
も著名だったが、リルケは「見る」ことについて
徹底的に考えた詩人である。外国語を日本語に移
しかえる時は、一つの影像を注意深く、しかも
「かすかに」見据えるという作業がたえず必要に
なる。この歌は、そんな習性がみごとに生かされ
た一例のような気がする。

Two peaches

draw together, rained on

by a spring

and dimly, through

the darkness, I am seeing. . . .

Takayasu Kuniyo

From *Gaijō* (On the Road, 1962). Reading this poem, you feel that you are actually there, gazing through the darkness at the peaches as a stream of water from a spring flows down over them. The effect is a little like an etching. The author was a well-known translator of Rilke, and Rilke was a poet who thought a great deal about the act of seeing. Transplanting a foreign language into Japanese is an operation that necessitates gazing at a single image with unwavering attention and yet "dimly," as if in mist, with an unfocused kind of sight. This poem is a beautiful application, I feel, of that way of seeing.

炎天の
Enten   no

遠き帆や
tōki   ho   ya

わが心の帆
waga   kokoro no   ho

山口誓子
Yamaguchi Seishi

『遠星』(昭二二)所収。明治三十四年京都生まれ
の俳壇の長老。見方によって青年のあこがれ心を
詠んだ青春の句とも、孤独な心境を遠い白帆に託
した述懐の句とも読める。俳句という短詩は作者
の真意を露骨に告げず、ふしぎに美しい、時を超
え心理を超えた世界を示すことがある、この句の
ように。実際には終戦一週間後の昭和二十年八月
二十二日の作。誓子は伊勢の海辺に病を養ってい
た。落魄といえば一番近いだろうような心境から
生まれた句だろう。

Distant sail

under blazing sun, sail

of my heart

Yamaguchi Seishi

From *Ensei* (Distant Star, 1947). Seishi, born 1901 in Kyoto, is one of the most respected poets in the haiku world today. Depending on one's point of view, one might call this either a poem of youth, in which a young person expresses longing, or else a poem of remembrance, in which an older person's sense of isolation is projected onto a sail seen far off in the distance. The brief haiku form, rather than conveying its creator's real meaning openly, sometimes, as here, shows us a strangely beautiful world beyond time and thought. In actual fact, this poem was written on August 22, 1945, one week after the end of the war, while Seishi was convalescing from illness near the sea at Ise. "Down and out" would probably best describe the mood it was born from.

川越えし
Kawa   koeshi

女の脛に
onna no hagi ni

花藻かな
hanamo   kana

高井几薫
Takai Kitō

『井華集』所収。几薫は与謝蕪村の高弟で、自選の『井華集』は天明俳壇屈指の句集。この句集に序文を書いているのは、几薫の親しい友だった無腸すなわち上田秋成で「巻をひらけば彩色まばゆきばかりなり」と絶讃した。川を歩いて渡った女の脛にまといつく藻の花、そのほのかな色気。几薫の師蕪村の「夏河を越すうれしさよ手に草履」とはおのずとまた別の官能のよろこびがある。彼は有名な酒徒で、書をよくし、句集板下も自筆だった。

A woman crossed the stream

and on her leg—

flowering riverweed!

Takai Kitō

From *Seikashū*. Kitō was Buson's chief disciple and this collection, which he edited himself, is one of the best of all late 18th century collections of haiku. The novelist Ueda Akinari, who was Kitō's close friend, contributed an enthusiastic preface under his haikai pen name of Muchō, saying: "When you open this book, its colors blind you with their brilliance." There is a faint eroticism to this picture of flowering riverweed clinging to the calf of a woman who has walked across a stream. "The pleasure/of crossing a summer stream!/Sandals in hand" (*natsukawa wo / kosu ureshisa yo / te ni zōri*), by Kitō's master Buson, expresses the joys of a different kind of sensuality. Kitō was a famous drinker and an accomplished calligrapher who prepared the manuscript for his collection in his own hand.

秋来ぬと
Aki kinu to

目にはさやかに
me ni wa sayaka ni

見えねども
mienedomo

風のおとにぞ
kaze no oto ni zo

おどろかれぬる
odorokarenuru

藤原敏行
Fujiwara Toshiyuki

『古今集』秋歌巻頭の立秋の歌。「おどろく」は
にわかに気づく。まだ目にはありありと見えない
が、ああもう風の音が秋をつげている。目に見え
るものより先に、「風」という「気配」によって
秋の到来を知るという発見が、この有名な歌のか
なめである。つまり「時」の移り行きを目ではな
く耳で聴き取る行き方で、より内面的な感じ方で
ある。これが後世の美学にも影響を与えたのだっ
た。

It's a fact: autumn's

here. To the eye it's still not

quite apparent, but

with the sound of the wind, I

suddenly became aware.

Fujiwara Toshiyuki

Kokinshū, the first poem on the coming of autumn. *Odoroku*: "to suddenly notice, become aware." Autumn changes are not clearly visible in the land-scape yet, but the sound of the wind announces the new season. The fulcrum of the poem is the discovery that before autumn becomes apparent to the eye, one knows of its arrival by the wind, which is a sign or portent. The flow of time, in other words, is perceived not by the eye but by the ear, in a very introspective mode of feeling. This had an influence on aesthetics even in later ages.

遺棄死体
Ikishitai

数百といひ
sūhyaku   to   ii

数千といふ
sūsen   to   iu

いのちをふたつ
inochi   wo   futatsu

もちしものなし
mochishi   mono   nashi

土岐善磨
Toki Zenmaro

『六月』(昭十五)所収。敗走する敵が遺棄した死
体は数百、あるいは数千にも達すると戦果を報じ
たニュースに対して、命を二つ持った人間などい
ないと、つぶやくごとく応じた歌。昭和十五年の
作で、当時発表するのに勇気を要した種類の歌だ
った。実際、上記歌集をもって非愛国的反戦思想
と攻撃する歌人も現れた。今読めば、歌集全体と
してはむしろ、迷いや悲しみの暗い調子が胸をう
つ。作者としてはおのれ自身への誠実を保つこと
だけが支えだったろう。

"Abandoned corpses numbered

in the hundreds," they say,

"in the thousands"

Not one of us

can live twice

Toki Zenmaro

From *Rokugatsu* (June, 1940). The war news announced that corpses abandoned by the defeated enemy numbered in the hundreds and thousands. The poet whispers back to this triumphant news that each of us has only one life, unique and irreplaceable. In 1940, at the height of World War II, it required courage to publish a poem like this. In fact, some of the author's fellow tanka poets did attack *Rokugatsu* as an expression of unpatriotic anti-war ideology. But reading its poems now, what strikes one throughout is, more than anything, the dark tone of confusion and sadness. The fact that Zenmaro remained true to himself as a writer must have been what sustained him.

AUTUMN POEMS

秋のうた

木のまより
Ko no ma yori

もりくる月の
morikuru tsuki no

影見れば
kage mireba

心づくしの
kokorozukushi no

秋は来にけり
aki wa kinikeri

よみ人しらず
Yomibito shirazu

『古今集』秋上。「心づくし」は心を尽くさせる
こと。秋になると野山の趣が変わってあちらにも
こちらにも美しく色づきはじめた自然界のすがた
がある。しかもそれらはたちまち過ぎ去ってゆく
つかのまの黄金の輝きである。それを思うたびに
気がもめる。それが「心づくしの秋」。こちらの
主観的な気分に重点をおいて、実は秋の情感を客
観的に深くとらえた含蓄ある表現が受け、『源氏
物語』その他にひろく愛用された。

When I look up and see

moonlight filter through the trees,

I know that autumn,

heart-exhausting autumn,

is already here

Anonymous

From *Kokinshū*, Autumn 1. *Kokorozukushi*: to use up one's heart, exhaust one's feelings. With autumn, the look of the fields and mountains changes. Here and there beautiful colors begin to dot the natural world. But this is a golden light that lasts but an instant and then is gone. Every time I think of it, says the poet, my heart is uneasy. That is *kokoro-zukushi*, "heart-exhausting autumn." Though stressing subjective emotion, the evocative phrase in fact captured the feel of autumn with deep objectivity and so won popularity. It was used in the *The Tale of Genji* and many other works later on.

秋風や
Akikaze ya

しらきの弓に
shiraki no yumi ni

弦はらん
tsuru haran

向井去来
Mukai Kyorai

『芭蕉七部集』中『曠野』所収の秋の句。芭蕉の
高弟。清雅な人柄の努力家で、武芸のたしなみが
あった。うるしも塗らず籐も巻かない白木の弓、
さわやかな秋風の白さそのままのこの弓に、弦を
張ってまとに真向かう緊張と快さ。作者の人柄を
ほうふつさせるためもあって去来の代表作となっ
た。夏目漱石は熊本の五高教師時代、俳句初心の
生徒、のちの科学者で漱石門の文人となる寺田寅
彦に句の心得を問われ、佳句の例としてこれをあ
げたという。

Autumn breeze—

Come, string a bow of

unvarnished wood!

Mukai Kyorai

An autumn poem from *Wild Fields* in the *Bashō Shichibu Shū*. Kyorai was one of Bashō's closest disciples. Elegant, genteel, and also hard working, he was accomplished in the martial arts. A bow of unvarnished wood, not even wound about with rattan—to its whiteness, fresh as the autumn breeze, he attaches a bowstring, and with intense pleasure aims straight at the target. In part because it hints at the author's own personality, this became Kyorai's best known poem. When Natsume Sōseki taught high school in Kumamoto, Terada Torahiko, then his student but later to become a scientist and also a member of Sōseki's literary circle, asked advice on how to compose haiku. Sōseki gave this poem as an example of what the beginner should strive for.

山里は
Yamazato   wa

松の声のみ
matsu no   koe   nomi

ききなれて
kikinarete

風ふかぬ日は
kaze   fukanu   hi   wa

寂しかりけり
sabishikarikeri

太田垣蓮月
Ōtagaki Rengetsu

『海女の刈藻』所収。寛政三年京都に生まれ、明治八年、八十五歳で没した歌人。四人の子が皆早世し、夫も蓮月三十歳の時に死んだ。以後は尼となって、陶器を焼いて生計をたてたが、独習の焼物の雅趣がかえって愛され、また多芸、美貌だったため、大いに名が喧伝された。しかし蓮月は好奇心で近づく俗客の訪問を嫌い、閑寂を求めて京の各地を転々、簡素に暮らした。虚飾なく詠じた歌の調べは優雅で、しんとした静けさが印象的。

In the mountain village

my ears know only

the voice of the pines—

windless days

are lonely

Ōtagaki Rengetsu

From *Ama no Karumo* (The Fishergirl's Seaweed).
A tanka poet, Rengetsu was born in Kyoto in 1791
and died 1875, aged 84. Her four children all died
young, and after she being widowed at 30 she
became a Buddhist nun. As a means of livelihood
she made pottery, a craft she had taught herself.
The artistry of her work, as well as her many talents
and her beauty, brought her great renown. She dis-
liked visitors drawn only by vulgar curiosity, however. To find peace and quiet, she moved about
from place to place in the Kyoto area, living simply.
The elegance of her unadorned style and the deep
peace of her poems leave a lasting impression.

夕星は
Yūzutsu wa

かがやく朝が八方に
kagayaku asa ga happō ni

散らしたものを
chirashita mono wo

みな
mina

もとへ
moto e

連れかへす。
tsurekaesu。

サッポー（呉　繁一訳）
Sapphō　　　　Kure Shigeichi

　　紀元前七世紀レスボス島に生まれた有名なギリシャ女流詩人の作中、わずかに残る短唱の一つ。上に続けて「羊をかへし　山羊をかへし　幼な子をまた母の手に連れかへす」と歌う。早く明治時代に上田敏による訳もある。夕暮れ、空に光り始める星の静かな輝き。「朝が八方に散らしたものを」再び集め束ねるものとして夕星をとらえているのが美しい。古代西洋の一女流詩人の見方だが、今もって新鮮である。

The evening star

leads home

to the beginning

all that shining morning scattered

to the eight directions

Sapphō (from the translation of Kure Shigeichi)

One of the few extant lyrics by the famous woman poet of Greece, born on the island of Lesbos in the seventh century before Christ. After the lines above she wrote, "It leads the sheep/leads the goat/leads home the child to her mother's hand" (*Hitsuji wo kaeshi / yagi wo kaeshi / osanago wo mata haha no te ni tsurekaesu*). This poem has been known in Japan since the Meiji period, thanks to the translation of Ueda Bin. The quiet glow of the stars begins to light up the sky at dusk. The image of the evening star gathering in and bringing together what "morning scattered to the eight directions" is beautiful. The vision of one woman, an ancient poet in a distant land, retains its freshness now.

星既に
Hoshi sude ni

秋の眼を
aki no manako wo

ひらきけり
hirakikeri

尾崎紅葉
Ozaki Kōyō

『紅葉山人俳句集』(明三七)所収。上記句集は明
治三十六年紅葉が没して後、瀬川疎山の編で刊行
された最初の紅葉句集。季語別に編集されていて、
八月「立秋」の項にこの句がある。まだ日中は暑
い日が続いているが、夜ともなれば空の星の光に
も変化が見える。その微妙な感じを言いとめて実
に新鮮な感覚の句。紅葉は西洋文学にも関心が深
かったが、この句にはまさに西洋浪漫派の詩の切
れ味がある。

The stars have already

opened

their autumn eyes

Ozaki Kōyō

From *Kōyō Sanjin Haiku Shū*, 1904. This was the first collection of Kōyō's haiku to be published. It was compiled after his death in 1903, by Segawa Sozan, who arranged the poems by season. The poem above comes under "Autumn begins," which is August. At this time of the year the days are still hot, but at night, under the light of the stars, one senses a change in the air. The poem achieves a sensation of real freshness by capturing this subtle feeling in words. Kōyō had read widely in Western literature; this poem has the vibrancy of Western Romantic poetry.

うたたねに
Utatane *ni*

恋しき人を
koishiki *hito* *wo*

見てしより
miteshi *yori*

夢てふものは
Yume *chō* *mono* *wa*

たのみそめてき
tanomi *someteki*

小野小町
Ono no Komachi

『古今集』巻十二恋二。六歌仙の一人で美人薄命
の代表とされるが、実際の詳しい伝は不明。哀切
優艶な実作を通じて面影をしのぶほかない。『古
今集』巻十二冒頭に三首並ぶ小町作の歌の一つ。
三首ともはかない夢の歌であるのは、編者たちの
意識的なはからいだったろう。恋しい人を夢で見
る時は実は相手がこちらを思っているからだ、と
いう当時の俗信を踏まえ、一度は夢で逢えたのに、
その後はたえて夢でさえ逢えない、という悲しみ
を余情としている。

Briefly I slept

and saw

the one I love

Now I place my faith

· in this thing called dreams

Ono no Komachi

Kokinshū, Book XII, Love 2. Komachi is considered one of the Six Poetic Immortals and an example of the misfortunes that beauty can bring. But in fact little is known of her life; the only records we have are her poignant and beautiful poems. Book XII of the *Kokinshū* begins with three poems by Komachi, of which this is one. All three are about brief dreams; doubtless the compilers planned this consciously. Komachi alludes to the then-popular belief that dreaming of the person you loved meant that he or she desired you. The poem's undercurrent is a lament that although she once met her lover in a dream, now he never comes, not even in dreams.

入れ替への
Irekae   no

催促に来る
saisoku   ni   kuru

赤とんぼ
akatonbo

誹風柳多留拾遺
Haifū Yanagidaru Shūi

　「入れ替へ」の語、現代人には何の事やらすぐに
は分かりかねるが、秋の到来とともにそわそわし
はじめ、質屋に入れていた冬物をそろそろ夏物と
入れ替えに請け出さねば、と感じる江戸庶民の生
活感を反映した言葉なのだ。トンボを見て「蜻蛉
やとりつきかねし草の上」と詠んだ芭蕉、「蜻蛉
や村なつかしき壁の色」と詠んだ蕪村とはまた別
の感覚でとらえたトンボの季節感が、川柳にはあ
ったわけである。

Come to press me

to redeem my winter clothes—

a red dragonfly

Haifū Yanagidaru Shūi

The word *irekae*, literally "substitution," has passed out of our vocabulary today, but in the Edo period it was an essential word in the life of the common people. When autumn arrived, people felt they had to take their winter clothes back from the pawn-broker and pawn their summer ones instead; *irekae* was the name for this process. Bashō wrote: "Dragonfly .../Unable to cling/to a blade of grass" (*tonbō ya/toritsuki kaneshi/kusa no ue*), and Buson wrote: "Dragonfly .../The color of the wall/reminds me of home" (*tonbō ya/mura natsukashiki/kabe no iro*). But for *senryū*, or satiric haiku, the dragonfly's seasonal associations, as seen here, were quite different.

留守と言え
Rusu   to   ie

ここには誰も居らぬと言え
Koko   ni wa dare mo   oranu   to   ie

五億年経ったら帰って来る
Go-oku nen   tattara   kaette   kuru

高橋新吉
Takahashi Shinkichi

『高橋新吉の詩集』(昭二四)所収。明治三十四年
愛媛県生まれの現代詩人。二十二歳の時『ダダイ
スト新吉の詩』を出し、日本最初のダダイスト詩
人となった。青年期に真言宗の寺で修行したが、
やがて禅に傾倒、「禅詩人」として海外でも知ら
れるにいたった。禅的契機をつかんではっしと対
象の本質を射とめたような詩が多い。これは「る
す」と題する三行詩で、代表作とされる。わずか
三行の中に、日常の時空を一挙に脱出する詩の魔
術がある。

Say I'm out   Say no one's here

In five hundred million years

I'll come home

Takahashi Shinkichi

From *Takahashi Shinkichi no Shishū*, 1949. Born in Ehime Prefecture, this modern poet died in 1987 at age 86. At 22 he published *Dadaisuto Shinkichi no Shi* (The Poems of Dadaist Shinkichi) and became the first Dadaist poet in Japan. When young he lived as a monk in a Shingon Buddhist temple, but later turned passionately to Zen Buddhism. His renown as "the Zen poet" even spread abroad. Many of his poems seize a Zen moment and instantly fly to the heart of the object. The title of this three-line poem, which is one of his most famous, is "Away from home." To escape everyday time and space at a stroke—this is poetry's magic, and these few lines possess it.

空をあゆむ
Sora wo ayumu

朗朗と月ひとり
rō-rō to tsuki hitori

荻原井泉水
Ogiwara Seisensui

『原泉』（昭三五）所収。昭和五十一年九十一歳で
没した東京生まれの俳人。明治四十四年師の河東
碧梧桐とともに新傾向の俳句誌「層雲」を創刊、
数年で自由律俳句に転じ、尾崎放哉、種田山頭火
ら自由律の俊才を育てた。句集、評論集など四百
冊はあろうという多産の人である。この句は大正
九年の作。月もひとりなら私もひとり、ひとりな
るがゆえに朗々と自由に歩む仲間、という気分だ
ろう。「朗朗と」に作者の大切な気持ちがある。

It walks the sky, cloudless,

clear: the moon alone

Ogiwara Seisensui

From *Gensen* (The Wellspring, 1960). Seisensui, a haiku poet born in Tokyo, died in 1976, aged 91. In 1911, with his haiku teacher Kawahigashi Heki-gotō, he began the magazine *Sōun* (Stratus Clouds), for publishing "new tendency" haiku. Some years later he shifted to "free-form haiku" and nurtured the talent of such poets as Ozaki Hōsai and Taneda Santōka. He was prolific, publishing about 400 volumes of verse and prose. This poem dates from 1920. The moon is alone. So am I. We walk together, one above and one below, each alone in freedom, bright and clear. *Rō-rō*, "cloudless, clear," is where the poem's emphasis lies.

鳰の海や
Nio no umi ya

月の光の
Tsuki no hikari no

うつろへば
utsuroeba

浪の花にも
nami no hana ni mo

秋は見えけり
aki wa miekeri

藤原家隆
Fujiwara no Ietaka

『新古今集』巻四秋歌上。「鳰の海」は琵琶湖の
こと。「浪の花」は白波を花にたとえた。湖水の
白波に忍び寄る秋を見ているのだが、調べの優美、
影像の清緻、さすが新古今代表歌人の作である。
この歌は『古今集』の文屋康秀の作、「草も木も
色かはれどもわたつみの波の花にぞ秋なかりけ
る」を踏んでいる。康秀が色の変わらぬ白波には
秋も冬もないといったのに対し、家隆が果たして
そうかと応じた形。両者の感覚表現の差は歴然と
している。

When the moon lights up

the Sea of Grebes

fall shows itself

even in the flowers

of the waves

Fujiwara no Ietaka

Shinkokinshū, Book IV, Autumn Poems 1. *Nio no umi*, "Sea of Grebes," is Lake Biwa. *Nami no hana,* "flowers of the waves," are whitecaps compared to flowers. The speaker is watching the subtle signs of autumn in the whitecaps on the lake. The rhythmic beauty and precise imagery mark this as the work of a major poet of the *Shinkokinshū*. The poem alludes to one by Fun'ya no Yasuhide in the *Kokin-shū*: "Grass and trees/change color/but for the whitecapped waves/upon the sea/there is no fall" (*kusa mo ki mo / iro kawaredomo / watatsu-umi no / nami no hana ni zo / aki nakarikeru*). Ietaka's poem is, in effect, a challenge to Yasuhide's assertion that there can be no fall or winter for the whitecaps whose color never changes. There is a striking difference between the two poets in how they sense and also express the world around them.

世の中に
Yo　no　naka　ni

こひしきものは
Koishiki　　　mono　　wa

はまべなる
hamabe　　　naru

さゞいのからの
sazai　　no　　kara　　no

ふたにぞありける
futa　　ni　　zo　　arikeru

良寛
Ryōkan

『近世和歌集・良寛』所収。「戯歌」と題する。
この世で何より恋しいものは、浜辺にころがる
蠑螺の殻の蓋だというのである。変なものを恋し
がったもので、それだけでも何かおかしいが、こ
の時の弟由之あての手紙では、「目ぐすり入の壺
のふたによろしく」と、海岸で適当なのを探して
くれるよう頼んでいる。サザエには立派な用途が
あったわけだ。その用途がまたなかなか面白いが、
この歌のような誇張法は、戯れ歌の有力な武器だ
った。

What I love most

in all the world

is the lid of the shell

of the turbo snail

that lives on the shore!

Ryōkan

From *Kinsei Wakashū, Ryōkan*. Titled "A Playful Poem." To pine for an odd thing like the turbo snail's lid is amusing in itself, but in a letter of this time Ryōkan asked his younger brother Yoshiyuki to search the beach for "a good lid for my eye medicine jar"—evidently he found the snail wonderfully useful. This, too, is rather humorous; but it was the element of exaggeration, as in this poem, through which the *zareuta* or playful poem achieved its effect.

かたへより
Katae　　　　yori

すこし退きて
sukoshi　　shirizokite

ながむれど
nagamuredo

みにくきものは
minikuki　　mono　wa

みにくかりけり
minikukarikeri

九條武子
Kujō Takeko

『薫染』（昭三）所収。柳原白蓮、原阿佐緒、岡本
かの子らと共に、大正期女性歌人中の異色だった
のがこの人。西本願寺法主大谷光尊の次女として
生まれた。美貌をうたわれたが、新婚の夫が多年
海外に出たまま帰国しないなど、結婚生活は不幸
だった。宗教活動への没入、関東大震災罹災後没
頭した社会事業への献身。四十歳で急逝するまで
の生涯は、秘めた悲しみに耐えつつ、外的には波
乱の一生だった。強い信念の歌である。没後刊の
代表歌集より。

Moving back a little

from the side, I tried

a second look—but

the thing that pained my eyes

had kept all its ugliness

Kujō Takeko

From *Kunsen*, 1928. Like Yanagihara Byakuren, Hara Asao, and Okamoto Kanoko, the author stands out as unique among the women tanka poets of the Taishō period. The second daughter of Ōtani Kōson, head priest of Nishi Honganji (and thus head of the Jōdō Shinshū sect), she was a famous beauty; but she married a man who went abroad soon after and did not return for many years, and in that and other ways her married life was most unfortunate. She immersed herself in religious activities, and after a disastrous experience in the Great Earthquake of 1923, dedicated herself to public welfare endeavors. Her life until she died at the young age of 40 was one of hidden sadness, endured alone, amid outer turmoil. This poem expresses strong conviction. *Kunsen*, published posthumously, is her most important collection.

空山　人を見ず
Kūzan　hito　wo　mizu

但だ人語の響きを聞く
tada　jingo　no　hibiki　wo　kiku

王維
Ōi

『唐詩選』所収。題は「鹿柴」。唐の大詩人王維は長安南郊の広大な別荘を入手し、敷地内の名勝二十を選んでそれぞれに命名した。「鹿柴」もそれで、この詩句はそこで味わう幽遠な情緒を詠んだ五言絶句の前半。「空山」は人の気配のない山。にもかかわらず、どこからともなく人の話し声が響いてくるのだ。だれにも覚えのある秋山の情景である。それにしても、日本人に愛読されるこの唐代自然詩人は大したお金持ちだったらしい。

Empty mountains see no people

hear only the echoes of human words

Wang Wei

From *Tōshi Sen*. The title is "The Deer Enclosure."
This great Chinese poet of the Tang dynasty acquired
a vast estate in the country south of Ch'ang-an and
selected twenty scenic spots in it, to each of which
he gave a name. These lines are the first half of a
poem in the *gogon sekku* form (four lines, five characters each), written to express the beauty of the spot
called "The Deer Enclosure." "Empty mountains,"
kūzan, means mountains without any sound or
trace of human beings. And yet, from somewhere
come the faint echoes of people speaking. This is a
scene in the autumn mountains that anyone might
have experienced. It's rather a surprise to learn that
this eighth century nature poet, so beloved in Japan,
was also extremely wealthy.

寂しさは
Sabishisa wa

その色としも
sono iro to shimo

なかりけり
nakarikeri

真木立つ山の
Maki tatsu yama no

秋の夕暮
aki no yūgure

寂蓮法師
Jakuren Hōshi

『新古今集』巻四秋上。新古今のいわゆる「三夕
の歌」の第一。「三夕の歌」は、秋の寂寥の底に
通常の美よりも一層深い美を見ている三首を並べ
ている。真木は杉・檜などの良材の総称、槇。秋
の色といえば紅葉というのがまずは常識である。
しかるにこの歌は、常緑の真木がしんと並び立つ
秋山の夕べに、どこがどうと特定できない(「その
色としもなき」)いわく言い難い寂寥相を見て、そ
のふかぶかとした美の幽玄味にうたれているので
ある。

Loneliness is not

a single

color:

Cypress covered mountains

in the autumn dusk

Priest Jakuren

Shinkokinshū, Book IV, Autumn 1. The first of the collection's so-called "Three evening poems," which see within autumn's loneliness a beauty even deeper than ordinary beauty. *Maki* is a general term for evergreens like cypress and cryptomeria. The phrase "autumn colors" usually brings to mind bright red and yellow leaves. But here evergreens stand silently on a mountain in the autumn dusk and the poet, seeing in them a loneliness whose source he can neither pinpoint nor define (*sono iro to shimo naki*), is struck by a profound and mysterious beauty.

芋嵐
Imoarashi

猫が鬚張り
Neko ga hige hari

歩きをり
arukiori

村山古郷
Murayama Kokyō

『村山古郷集』(昭五五)所収。明治四十二年京都
市生まれの俳人・俳論家。同じく俳人だった兄葵
郷の手ほどきで俳句を始めた。近代俳句・俳壇史
の知見の広さでは定評があり、その方面での著作
も多い。いもの葉裏を白くひるがえらせて吹く強
い秋風が「芋嵐」。この秋風が吹くころには、初
夏ごろ生まれた子猫たちもりっぱに一人前になっ
ている。ひげをぴんと張って畑中の道をゆく猫の、
いかにも威厳ありげな姿のもつおかしみ。

Taro wind—

whiskers extended,

the cat walks on

Murayama Kokyō

From *Murayama Kokyō Shū*, 1980. Haiku poet and critic born 1909 in Kyoto, died 1986 in Tokyo. He began writing haiku under the guidance of his elder brother Kikyō, also a haiku poet. Respected for the breadth of his knowledge of modern haiku history and its groups, he published many books in those areas too. *Imoarashi* is the strong autumn wind that blows the taro leaves back so that their white undersides show. When this wind blows, the kittens born in early summer are turning into handsome adult cats. The sight of one of them walking, whiskers extended, on the paths through the fields with that special dignity cats have, has *okashimi* or the humor characteristic of haiku.

金烏西舎に臨らひ
Kin'u　seisha　ni　terai

鼓声短命を催す
Kosei　tanmei　wo　unagasu

泉路賓主無し
Senro　hinshu　nashi

此の夕家を離りて向かふ
Kono　yūbe　ie　wo　sakarite　mukau

大津皇子
Ōtsu no Miko

　現存最古の日本漢詩集『懐風藻』所収。天武帝
皇子で文武にひいで、詩も和歌も抜群の天分を示
したという。天武帝崩御後の皇位継承の有力候補
だったが、反逆罪の汚名のもとに謀殺された。二
十四歳の臨終の詩。「金烏」は太陽。「泉路」は死
出の旅路。日は傾いて西の家を照らし、夕べの時
を告げる鼓は私の短い命をさらにせきたてるよう
に響く。よみ路には客も主人もない。私はただ独
り、家を去って遠い旅に立つのだ。

The golden crow lights the houses in the west

And drumbeats hurry my short life on

There are no hosts or guests on

   the road to death:

Tonight I leave my home, to venture there

                              Ōtsu no Miko

From *Kaifūso*, the oldest extant collection of Chinese verse made in Japan. The author, son of Emperor Tenmu, was gifted in the arts of peace and war, with a special talent for poetry. After the death of his father, he was one of the leading contenders for the kingship, but was executed on suspicion of fomenting rebellion. This poem was written on the last day of his life. *Kin'u*, "golden crow," is the sun. The sun sets, its light spreading west, and the drum that announces night echoes as though further hastening the end of my short life. There are no companions on the road to death, "no hosts or guests." Alone, I leave my home and set off on that distant journey.

こほろぎの
Kōrogi *no*

音は地より湧く
ne *wa* *chi* *yori* *waku*

臥て聴けば
Nete *kikeba*

あをまつむしは
Aomatsumushi *wa*

天より下る
ame *yori* *kudaru*

上田三四二
Ueda Miyoji

『鎮守』(平元)所収。著者の死の直後に出た最終歌集の一首。すでに死を覚悟した身である。見回すすべてが芥川龍之介の言葉にいう、澄んだ「末期の眼」のもとに見られている。秋の虫の声は地から湧き、天から下る。それを聴き分ける耳も、すでに地の下、また天上にある。「臥て聴けば」を真ん中に置いた所に、作者の技術のこまやかさがある。これを初句に置いても意味だけなら変わらない。

The black cricket's song

wells up from the earth

—I lie awake and listen—

The green pine cricket

comes down from heaven

Ueda Miyoji

From *Chinju*, 1989. This was the author's last tanka collection, published just after his death. In this poem, he had already made his peace with death. Everything that he saw as he looked around him had the clarity offered, in Akutagawa Ryūnosuke's phrase, to "the eyes in life's last moments." The voices of the autumn insects well up from the earth and descend from the sky. The ears that can tell the difference are already both under the earth and high in the sky. Making "I lie awake and listen," *nete kikeba*, the precise center of the poem shows the poet's meticulous artistry. As far as meaning alone goes, it could just as well have been made the first line.

病雁の
Byōgan　no

夜さむに落て
yosamu　ni　ochite

旅ね哉
tabine　kana

松尾芭蕉
Matsuo Bashō

『猿蓑』所収。「堅田にて」と前書。異本では「かただにふしなやみて」ともある。元禄三年晩秋、近江湖畔の堅田で旅寝した時の作。芭蕉は折悪しく体調も崩していたが、冷たい粗末な寝床に横たわる彼の心の目に、夜空から一羽の病気の雁が落下してくる幻が見えたのである。その雁と芭蕉自身が、一瞬二にして一となる、深沈たる夜の光景。「夜さむに落ちて」が「旅ね哉」へ転じる呼吸は、まさに至芸というほかない。

Ill, a wild goose falls

cold in the night—

the traveler's sleep

Matsuo Bashō

From *Sarumino* (The Monkey's Raincoat). The headnote says "At Katada." A variant text has "At Katada, lying in pain." The poem was written late in the autumn of 1670, when Bashō spent the night at Katada on Lake Biwa while on a journey. He lay on his cold and spartan bed, feeling unwell, and to his mind's eye came the vision of a wild goose, sick and falling through the night sky. For an instant, the bird and Bashō himself seemed to be a single being, joined in the depths of a hushed night. The rhythm of the poem's shift from *yosamu ni ochite*, "falls/cold in the night," to *tabine kana*, "the traveler's sleep," is artistic perfection itself.

風きけば
Kaze   kikeba

嶺の木の葉の
mine no   konoha   no

中空に
nakazora ni

吹き捨てられて
fuki   suterarete

落つる声々
otsuru   koegoe

正徹
Shōtetsu

『草根集』所収。僧にして室町初期を代表する歌人なる正徹は、元来備中国神戸山城主の子だった。十歳ごろ父母と共に上京し、十代半ばから京都歌壇の歌会にも出席していたという。のち出家したが、歌に歌論に大活躍し、心敬ら連歌作者多数を門下に擁した。文人僧輩出の室町という時代を身をもって示した人である。歌数四万という多産さだが、歌風はこの歌にも見られるように、遥かなものに耳を澄まして、細やかに歌いわけ、しかも余情深いものがある。

I hear the wind

in the mountain trees

and the voices of the leaves

blown through air

then let go, falling

Shōtetsu

Sōkonshū (Grass Roots). Shōtetsu, a Buddhist priest and leading tanka poet of the early Muromachi period, was born in the province of Bitchū, the son of the lord of Kōdoyama. When he was about 10, he and his parents moved to Kyoto. By his teen, he was participating in tanka workshops held by recognized poets in Kyoto. Though he later took monastic vows, he was a very active poet and critic, and took many renga poets, including Shinkei, under his wing. He is an excellent example of the many poet-priests of the Muromachi period. A prolific poet, he is said to have written 40,000 tanka. As this poem shows, his style, with its close attention to such subtle events as the far-off sound of the wind, was capable of creating deep overtones.

つぶらなる
Tsubura naru

汝が眼吻はなん
na ga me suwanan

露の秋
Tsuyu no aki

飯田蛇笏
Iida Dakotsu

　『山盧集』（昭七）所収。大正三年二十九歳の作。
当時蛇笏には、芥川龍之介を感嘆させた「死病え
て爪うつくしき火桶かな」の繊美な句があったが、
上のような純情可憐な句もあった。「吻」の字は
口さき、唇の意で吸う意はない。「吻はなん」も
本来は「吻ひなん」で、共に厳密には誤用だろう。
しかし「汝が眼吻ひなん」ではぶちこわしになる
のが詩の不思議。接吻を連想させつつ「眼」のこ
としか言わない所、純情句だが手腕はしたたか。

Your full, round

eyes I'll sip—

Dewy autumn

Iida Dakotsu

From *Sanroshū* (Mountain Hut, 1932). Written in 1914, at age 29. In the same year Dakotsu wrote this beautiful haiku, which deeply impressed Akutagawa Ryūnosuke: "Mortally ill/her fingernails so beauti-ful/on the brazier" (*Shibyō ete/tsume utsukushiki/hioke kana*). But he also wrote poems of artless puri-ty, like the one above. The character 吻 means "lip," not "sip." *Suwanan* should properly be *suinan*. So, strictly speaking, there are two mistakes. However, if they were corrected to *suinan* 吸ひなん the effect —and this is the wonder of poetry—would be ruined. The poem speaks only of eyes yet makes us imagine a kiss: artful technique serves artless emo-tion.

雲霞
Kumo kasumi

呑つゝ越ん
nomitsutsu　　*koen*

菊の山路
kiku　no　yamaji

田上菊舎
Tagami Kikusha

『手折菊』所収。宇治の万福寺で詠んだ「山門を出れば日本ぞ茶摘唄」で有名な女流俳人。長州藩士の家に生まれ、二十四歳で夫に死別、以後七十四で死ぬまで、江戸後期俳壇の女流としては破格の活動的で多彩な生涯を送った。旅に明け旅に暮れ、七弦琴も漢詩も、また書・画・茶道、すべてに秀で、もし現代に生きていたらと空想せずにはいられない女性である。上の句も、旅を詠んで大らかに意気軒昂。

Swallowing clouds and

mist, I cross the mountainways,

all chrysanthemums

Tagami Kikusha

From *Taorigiku*. A female haiku poet, famous for "I walk out the temple gate/and it's Japan!/The teapickers' song" (*sanmon wo / dereba nihon zo / chatsumiuta*), written about coming back to everyday Japanese life from the cloistered world of Uji's Manpuku Temple, which was built totally in Ming Chinese style. Born into a samurai family of the Chōshū domain, Kikusha was widowed at 24; from then until she died at age 74, she led a varied and unconventional life as a woman in the haiku world of the late Edo period. She traveled constantly, and was admired for her skill at the seven-stringed koto and Chinese verse, as well as at calligraphy, painting and the tea ceremony. It is tempting to imagine what she would be doing if she lived now. This haiku about travel has her characteristic forward-looking energy and high spirits.

蝶老て
Chō *oite*

たましひ菊に
tamashii *kiku* *ni*

あそぶ哉
asobu *kana*

榎本星布
Enomoto Seifu

『星布尼句集』所収。晩秋の蝶が力なく菊に戯れ
ながら翔んでいる。死期も近い蝶のその飛翔を、
魂がうつつなく菊に遊んでいると見てとったので
ある。鋭い感覚の中に、老いを感じそめた自らの
身を晩秋の蝶になぞらえている気配も見えて哀れ
ふかい。作者は武蔵国八王子の本陣の娘で、若く
して夫と死別、尼になり、俳諧を俊才加舎白雄に
学んで抜きんでた女流俳人となった。「ゆく春や
蓬が中の人の骨」という異色作は有名。

The butterfly grown old

its spirit plays

among chrysanthemums

Enomoto Seifu

From *Seifu-ni Kushū*. At autumn's end, a butterfly
flutters weakly among the chrysanthemums. The
flight of this creature so close to death suggests a
ghost playing dreamily among the flowers. One
feels that the poet, with her keen sensitivity, has
become aware of her own aging and is comparing
herself to the butterfly; this creates deep pathos.
Seifu was the daughter of the leading innkeeper of
Hachiōji in Musashino Province, at whose estab-
lishment the great provincial lords stayed on their
trips back and forth to the capital. Widowed early,
she became a Buddhist nun, studied haiku with the
brilliant Kaya Shirao, and eventually became the
leading female haiku poet of her day. She is famous
for the following haiku, with its highly unusual
subject: "The passing spring!/Among the mugwort,
/human bones" (*yuku haru ya / yomogi ga naka no /
hito no hone*).

つつましき
Tsutsumashiki

儀式のごとく
gishiki　no　gotoku

朝なさな
asanasana

林檎一箇を
ringo　ikko　wo

夫とわかてり
tsuma　to　wakateri

川村ハツエ
Kawamura Hatsue

『孔雀青』（平六）所収。第三歌集だが、同時に英語TANKAの創作・研究でも中心的な立場にいる人。『TANKAの魅力』を最近刊行、これにより二つの賞を受けた。アストン、チェンバレン、ウェーリーらの日本文学史、古典詩歌論の訳者としてもすぐれた業績がある。「下北のひばのまな板買ひし夜はしづかに秋の水流しをり」などの作を見ても、生活を大事にする仕方が、地についている感じがする。

Each morning

in humble ceremony

between us we

divide a single apple:

my husband and I

Kawamura Hatsue

From *Kujakuao*, 1994. This is the third collection of tanka in Japanese by a writer who occupies a central position in both the creation and study of tanka in English. For her most recent book, *Tanka no Miryoku* (The Appeal of the English Tanka), she received two prizes. She has also made notable contributions as a translator of Aston's and Chamberlain's histories of Japanese literature and Waley's critical works on classical Japanese poetry. Another tanka by her is: "I bought a chopping board/of cypress from Shimokita/and at night/ the autumn water quietly/flowed down its sides" (*shimokita no/hiba no manaita/kaishi yo wa/shizuka ni aki no/mizu nagashi ori*). Her poetry combines a reverence for everyday life with a refreshingly down-to-earth feeling.

薄紅葉
Usumomiji

恋人ならば
Koibito   naraba

烏帽子で来
eboshi   de ko

三橋鷹女
Mitsuhashi Takajo

『魚の鰭』(昭十六)所収。自分が好きな作品を読めば、おのずと作者の人柄まであれこれ空想したくなる。だれにも覚えのある読者の楽しみだろうが、鷹女もそんな思いを刺戟する俳人の一人である。「薄紅葉」を見やりながら「恋人ならば烏帽子で来」(「来」は命令形、おいで)とつぶやいているのは、教養豊かに気位あくまで高く、妖艶でまたお茶目な悍馬のたおやめといったところか。彼女の肖像写真にもその感じが漂っている。

Pale red leaves:

If you're to be my lover

come in a tall silk hat

Mitsuhashi Takajo

Uo no Hire (The Fish's Fins, 1941). When I like a poem, I find myself imagining what the author is like, even how she or he looks. This is one of the pleasures of reading that everyone must have experienced at one time or another, and Takajo is a haiku poet who often inspires it. Perhaps that whispered command made while gazing on the red-tinged maple leaves comes from a high-spirited young woman who combines learned and lofty refinement with playful sensuality. Takajo's photographs convey the same feeling.

秋風や
Akikaze   ya

むしりたがりし
Mushiri-tagarishi

赤い花
akai   hana

小林一茶
Kobayashi Issa'

『おらが春』所収。前書に「さと女三十五日墓」
とある。文政二年、生後四百日で疱瘡のため死ん
だ長女さとの三十五日の墓参の句である。赤い花
をむしりたがったのは、もちろん死んだこの子。
表現の上ではそれが伏せられているため、かえっ
て茫然と悲しい親の気持ちが伝わるようだ。一茶
は二年前、生後わずか一ヵ月の長男を死なせてい
たため、さとを溺愛した。その子もまた運命の手
にむしり取られた。

The autumn wind . . .

She always wanted to pluck

the red flowers

Kobayashi Issa

From *Ora ga Haru* (The Year of My Life). The prefatory note says: "Sato's grave 35 days after her death." Issa wrote this haiku when he visited the grave of his first daughter Sato, who died of small-pox in 1819 when she was only one year and one month old. Seeing the bright red flowers, he remembered how she had always wanted to pluck them. In the original Japanese, the subject of *mushiri-tagarishi* "wanted to pluck," is unspecified, which, paradoxically, conveys the father's dazed sadness all the more strongly. Having lost his first son two years earlier, just one month after birth, Issa had doted on Sato. And then she too was plucked away by the hand of fate.

WINTER POEMS 冬のうた

君かへす
Kimi　kaesu

朝の鋪石
asa　no　shiki-ishi

さくさくと
zaku-saku　to

雪よ林檎の
Yuki　yo　ringo　no

香のごとくふれ
ka　no　gotoku　fure

北原白秋
Kitahara Hakushū

『桐の花』（大二）所収。明治末年、二冊の詩集
『邪宗門』『思ひ出』で近代詩史に新時代を画した
白秋は『桐の花』で歌人としても時の人となった。
新風という意味でも、また『桐の花』哀傷篇で歌
われているような、人妻との恋による未決監拘置
事件という一身上の大変化という意味でも、時の
人だった。「雪の夜の紅きゐろりにすり寄りつ人
妻とわれと何とすべけむ」。しかしもとより掲出
歌のような歌の中に彼の新風はあった。天性の五
官の清新、軽やかな輝き。

I send you home

in the morning, the snowy path

crunches under your feet

Oh snow, fall with

the scent of apples!

Kitahara Hakushū

From *Kiri no Hana* (Paulownia Flowers, 1913). In the late Meiji period, Hakushū defined a new era in modern poetry with his collections *Jashūmon* and *Omoide*; with *Kiri no Hana* he also became a central figure in tanka. This was not only because of its new style, but also because of the metamorphosis (recorded in the "Poems of Sorrow" section of *Kiri no Hana*) in his personal life that came about because of his arrest for having an adulterous affair: "A snowy night,/we draw near/the red hearth,/another's wife and I—/where can we go from here?" (*yuki no yo no / akaki irori ni / suriyoritsu / hitozuma to ware to / nan to subekemu*) But the real newness of his style was in poems like the one above. An innate freshness of the senses, an effortless luminosity.

おもひかね
Omoikane

妹がり行けば
imogari　　yukeba

冬の夜の
fuyu　no　yo　no

川風寒み
kawakaze　samumi

千鳥なくなり
chidori　　nakunari

紀　貫之
Ki no Tsurayuki

『拾遺集』巻四冬。『歌よみに与ふる書』で『古今集』や貫之をこきおろした正岡子規が「此歌ばかりは趣味ある面白き歌に候」としている歌だが、これは子規の短見。貫之には他にいい歌がいくらもある。この歌、元来は屏風絵に合わせた注文制作の歌である。冬・寒い川風・千鳥・恋人のもとへ急ぐ男という組み合わせが、いわば一つの典型的情景を演出し、やがて千鳥が冬の季語となる端緒の一つをもなした。「妹がり」は恋人の所へ。

Love-possessed, I went

to seek my sister

in the winter night

and the river wind blew cold

carrying the plovers' cries

Ki no Tsurayuki

From *Shūishū*, Book IV, Winter. Masaoka Shiki's *Utayomi ni atauru sho* (Letters to a Tanka Poet) was, among other things, a scathing denunciation of the *Kokinshū* and Tsurayuki, and in it Shiki wrote about this poem: "It is the only one [Tsurayuki wrote] that has any charm or interest." Shiki was, however, mistaken: Tsurayuki wrote many other fine poems. This particular one was written to order, to describe a painted screen. Winter, a cold river wind, plovers, and a man hurrying to his lover's house—the scene Tsurayuki presented here was to become almost an archetype in classical poetry, and, at the same time, one of the first steps on the way to "plovers" becoming a season word for winter. *Imogari* means "to where my lover is."

めざめして
Mezame shite

眼をあけず聴く
me wo akezu kiku

幽けさは
kazokesa wa

時雨の雨の
shigure no ame no

ふり出でぬらむ
furi-idenuramu

岡　麓
Oka Fumoto

『冬空』（昭二五）所収。雨は日本の詩歌の中で好んで詠まれた題材。「つくづくと独りきく夜の雨の音は降りをやむさへ寂しかりけり」は花園天皇皇女儀子内親王の歌。「楠の根を静にぬらす時雨かな」は蕪村の句。詩人たちの好みは、豪雨よりは細雨にいつも傾いた。名筆家で知られたこのアララギ派歌人最晩年の歌も、「幽けさ」をとらえて精妙。現代の細みある雨の名歌の一つだろう。

Awake,

eyes closed,

I listen. . . . that faintness

must be winter rain

begun to fall

Oka Fumoto

From *Fuyuzora* (Winter Sky, 1950). Rain has always been a popular subject in Japanese poetry. There is the tanka of Princess Gishi Naishinnō, a daughter of Emperor Hanazono: "Vacantly listening/alone at night/to the rain's sound,/even the lulls/are lonely" (*Tsukuzuku to / hitori kiku yo no / ame no ne wa / furi wo yamu sae / sabishikarikeri*). And there is Buson's haiku: "Winter rain/silently wets / the camphor tree's roots" (*Kusu no ne wo / shizuka ni nurasu / shigure kana*). Poets have always preferred misty drizzles to heavy downpours. This tanka, written near the end of his life by a member of the Araragi tanka group who was also a noted calligrapher, captures the quality of "faintness" with exquisite subtlety. It is one of the finest modern tanka on the thin rain of early winter.

星を数ふれば七つ、
Hoshi wo kazoureba nanatsu,

金の灯台は九つ、
kin no tōdai wa kokonotsu,

岩蔭に白き牡蛎かぎりなく
iwakage ni shiroki kaki kagirinaku

生るれど、
umaruredo,

わが恋はひとつにして
waga koi wa hitotsu ni shite

寂し。
sabishi.

西条八十
Saijō Yaso

『砂金』(大八)所収。明治二十五年東京生まれ、昭和四十五年没の詩人。童謡、歌謡曲、軍歌の作詞家としてあまりにも有名だが、元来繊細な言語感覚で心象のゆらめきをたくみにとらえて歌う、いわゆる大正期芸術派詩人の代表格の一人だった。これは短詩「海にて」の全文。「七つ」「九つ」「かぎりなく」、そして「わが恋はひとつ」と、数字の配置・対比を軸にして、恋と郷愁の情緒を歌う。しゃれた感覚の歌いぶり中に、古歌謡の骨法が生かされていて面白い。

Count the stars: there are seven.

And of gold lighthouses, nine.

In the shadows of the rocks,

white oysters breed, infinitudes,

but of my love there is but one,

alone.

Saijō Yaso

From *Sakin* (Gold Dust, 1919). A poet who was born in 1892 in Tokyo and died in 1970. Very famous as a lyricist for children's and popular and military songs. His works trace the subtle movements of the heart with a delicate and precise sense of language; he was one of the central figures among the so-called "artistic" poets of the Taisho period. This is the short poem "By the sea" in its entirety. "Seven," "nine," "infinitudes," "of my love there is but one"—the fulcrum is the placement and contrast of numerals as he sings of love and nostalgia. In his witty and sensitive style, he revivified a structural method sometimes found in old folk songs.

虫の卵を
Mushi no tamago wo

育ててゐたる
sodatete itaru

冬の芝
fuyu no shiba

長谷川かな女
Hasegawa Kanajo

『雨月』(昭十四)所収。かな女は高浜虚子が力を
入れて育成した「ホトトギス」婦人句会(大正二
年以降)で、最初から頭角を現した人だった。大
正三年の作「羽子板の重きが嬉し突かで立つ」を
虚子が賞揚したのは有名で、実際それが彼女の代
表作ともなった。「虫の卵」の句は、その二十数
年後の作だが、さりげない描写によって、隠れた
所で持続する生命力への賛美を詠みこんでいるの
が印象的。

Parent to

the insects' eggs—

the winter lawn

Hasegawa Kanajo

From *Ugetsu* (Moon in the Rain, 1939). Kanajo was from the beginning the leading figure in the *Hoto-togisu* Women's Haiku Society, which Takahama Kyoshi worked hard to establish and nurture from 1913 on. Kyoshi's praise of her 1914 haiku "The battledore's/heavy weight is my delight—/I stand still, not striking" (*hagoita no/omoki ga ureshi/tsukade tatsu*) is well known, and that poem in fact became her best known work. She wrote the "insects' eggs" haiku about twenty years later. What is impressive about it is that she makes a seemingly casual descrip-tion into a homage to the life force that endures in hidden places.

こしかた ゆくすゑ
Koshikata *yukusue*

雪あかりする
yuki *akari* *suru*

種田山頭火
Taneda Santōka

　『草木塔』（昭十五）所収。波乱の前半生ののち出
家得度した山頭火は、大正末年から昭和十五年の
死の直前にいたるまで、日本中を一笠一杖の身で
漂泊しつづけた。これは十四年十二月半ば、松山
市に仮寓一草庵を得てやっと定住した時の句で、
「帰居」と前書きする。来し方も行く末も茫洋、
しかしそこに窓の雪あかりに似たほのかな光がさ
している、と。一草庵に入って十ヵ月後、彼は死
んだ。

The past, the future—

snowlight faintly glows

Taneda Santōka

From *Sōmokutō* (Grass and Tree Pagoda, 1940).
After a troubled and stormy youth, Santōka in middle age became a Buddhist priest. From 1925 until
shortly before he died in 1940, he roamed Japan as a
begging monk. This haiku, titled "Return," is from
mid-December, 1939, when he had finally settled
down in Matsuyama City in a little house he called
"A Blade of Grass." The past and the future, it
hints, are boundless and vast, but a faint light shines
on both, like the dim glow given off by snow at
night. Ten months after moving into A Blade of
Grass, Santōka died.

すでにすでに
Sude ni sude ni

冬日を鼻に
fuyuhi wo hana ni

おん屍
onkabane

石塚友二
Ishizuka Tomoji

『光塵』(昭二九)所収。昭和二十二年歳晩、小説家横光利一が逝去した。作者は横光に師事した作家・俳人で、これは「今生に師なし」と題する追悼句の一つ。五十年近くを息づいてきた鼻孔に、いま冬日が落ち、人ははや「おん屍」になってしまった。生者が死者に変る厳粛な瞬間をとらえて悲痛な実感がある。飯田蛇笏に「死骸や秋風かよふ鼻の穴」という忘れ難い一句があるが、それを思い出させる。

So soon, so soon

the winter sun on its nose—

my teacher's corpse

Ishizuka Tomoji

From *Kōjin*, 1954. In late 1947, the novelist Yoko-mitsu Riichi died. Tomoji, a writer of fiction and haiku, had been his follower. This is one of several haiku of mourning he wrote under the title "In this world, I have no teacher." The winter sun is strik-ing nostrils that breathed in and out for nearly fifty years; the person has already become a corpse. With a sense of tragic realization, the poem grasps that solemn instant when life crosses the border into death. I am reminded of Iida Dakotsu's memorable haiku: "Dead body—/ Autumn breezes blow/ through its nostrils" (*nakigara ya / akikaze kayou / hana no ana*).

心がうらぶれたときは
Kokoro ga　　　uraburreta　　　toki　　wa

音楽を聞くな。
ongaku　wo　kiku　na.

空気と水と石ころ
Kūki　to　mizu to　ishikoro

ぐらいしかない所へ
gurai　shika　nai　tokoro　e

そっと沈黙を食べに行け！
sotto　chinmoku wo　tabe　ni　ike.

清岡卓行
Kiyooka Takayuki

『四季のスケッチ』(昭四一)所収。大正十一年大
連生まれの詩人・作家。四行詩「耳を通じて」の
三行目半ばまで。「遠くから／生きるための言葉
が、谺してくるから。」という重要な結語があと
に続く。心うらぶれた時は音楽に慰めを求めに行
くな、むしろ荒野にそっと沈黙を食べに行け、と
いう。逆説ではない。うらぶれに徹することによ
り「言葉」の再生に賭けようという願いである。
ちなみに作者はその詩や小説でも知られるよう
に、大の音楽好き。

When your heart's in ruins,

never listen to music.

Go off somewhere there's nothing

but air, water, and stones,

and make a quiet meal of silence!

Kiyooka Takayuki

From *Shiki no Suketchi* (Sketches of the Four Seasons, 1966). A poet and prose writer born in Dairen, China, 1922. This is the first two and a half lines of the four line poem "Through the Ears." It goes on to these conclusive words: "Because from the distance come/echoes of the words that will help you live." (*tōku kara / ikiru tame no kotoba ga, kodama shite kuru kara.*) The poet is saying not to seek solace in music when one is depressed, but rather to go into the wilds and quietly eat silence. There is no paradox here. You give yourself up to sadness and await the rebirth of the necessary words. Kiyooka, by the way, as is evident from his poems and stories, loves music.

あなたまあ
Anata　*maa*

おかしな一生
okashina　*issho*

でしたねと
deshita　*ne*　*to*

会はば言ひたし
awaba　*iitashi*

父といふ男
chichi　*to*　*iu*　*otoko*

斎藤　史
Saitō Fumi

『渉りかゆかむ』(昭六〇)所収。「父」とは陸軍少
将、佐佐木信綱門の歌人斎藤瀏。二・二六事件で
反乱幇助罪に問われ、官位勲功すべてを失った。
二十代半ばだった作者は、この事件によって深刻
な影響を受けた。「白きうさぎ雪の山より出でて
来て殺されたれば眼を開き居り」という後年の彼
女の絶唱も、そういう経験を克服してきた人でな
ければ詠めない種類の歌だったといえそうに思
う。

Well, you have to

admit you had a pretty

weird life—that's

what I'll say if I bump into

the man I call father

Saitō Fumi

From *Watarika Yukamu*, 1985. "Father" was the Major General and tanka poet Saitō Ryū, a disciple of Sasaki Nobutsuna. He was accused of aiding the attempted coup d'etat of February 26, 1936 and stripped of all rank and honors. This revolt had a deep influence on his daughter, then in her mid-twenties. At the same time, I suspect that had she not overcome this experience, she could never have written the superb poems of her later years such as "A white rabbit, come/out from the snowbound mountains,/was killed, and that is/why its eyes are now/wide open" (*shiroki usagi / yuki no yama yori / idete kite / korosaretareba / me wo hiraki ori*).

咳の子の
Seki no ko no

なぞなぞあそび
nazonazo   asobi

きりもなや
kiri   mo   naya

中村汀女
Nakamura Teijo

『汀女句集』(昭十九)所収。女性俳人は今日きわ
めて多いが、家庭の主婦たることと句作りとを最
も幸福な形で調和させ得た俳人といえば、まずこ
の作者だろう。わが子を詠んだ句が多い上にすぐ
れてもいるのは、その事実と結びついた事といえ
る。風邪をひいて寝ている子が、相手になるよう
母親にせがみせがみ、なぞなぞ遊びに夢中になっ
ている。せきこみながら、それでもいつまでもや
めないのだ。

My coughing child's

riddle games

know no end

Nakamura Teijo

From *Teijo Kushū*, 1944. There are many, many female haiku poets today, but Teijo must be the best example of one who was able to harmonize in the happiest way the demands of family life and poetry. The fact that many of her best poems were about her own children was related to this. A sick child in bed begs his mother to play with him and forgets himself in telling riddles one after another. He goes on and on even while coughing.

里へ出る
Sato   e   deru

鹿の背高し
Shika no se takashi

雪明り
Yukiakari

炭　太祇
Tan Taigi

『太祇句選』所収。雪に埋もれた山中から餌を求
めて里に出てくる飢えた鹿。用心深く人家の周辺
に近づいてくる鹿の様子が、雪明かりの中にとら
えられている。意外なほど背が高いので、痛々し
いような思いさえ誘われる。太祇は人事句の名手
だが、こういう自然界の描写でも実にいい目をし
ていた。「川澄むや落葉の上の水五寸」などでも、
水底の落ち葉をとらえる俳人としての目の鋭さは
群を抜く。

Into the village

ventures a deer—so tall

in the snow-light!

Tan Taigi

From *Taigi Kusen*. A starving deer comes down from the snowbound mountains to forage for food. The poem captures it, visible in the light reflected off the snow, as it enters the village and cautiously edges near a house. Because it looks surprisingly tall, the sight is almost heart-wrenching. Taigi excelled at haiku about human events, but he was also superb at descriptions of the natural world like this one. Another haiku, about autumn leaves beneath flowing water, has the same extraordinary acuteness of observation: "How clear the river—/ five inches of water/above fallen leaves" (*kawa sumu ya / ochiba no ue no / miza gosun*).

過去は運に
Kako   wa un ni

けふは枯野に
kyō   wa kareno ni

躓けり
tsumazukeri

鈴木真砂女
Suzuki Masajo

『都鳥』(平六)所収。銀座の路地で小料理屋を営
む作者は、米寿を迎えてなお元気に店を切り盛り
しており、近来人気抜群というべき俳人であろう。
上記は八十八歳を記念して出した新句集だが、俳
句がそのまま日常の起居に溶けこんでしまったよ
うな境涯に達している。この句初五は、作者がか
つて経験した恋の有為転変をさしているのだろう
が、下句の軽みある表現は自在。「枯野に躓けり」
に飄逸な笑いがある。

In the old days it was

fate, today it's a withered

field that trips me up

Suzuki Masajo

From *Miyakodori* (Bird of the Capital), 1994. The author runs a small restaurant on a side-street off the Ginza. Still actively cooking for it in her late eighties, she is also one of the most popular of contemporary haiku poets. The collection that contains the haiku above was published to commemorate her eighty-eighth birthday. It attains a level where one feels there is no perceptible division between her poetry and her everyday life. The first line must refer to her shifting fortunes in the game of love, but the lightness of the last two lines takes us into another, freer realm entirely. There is a detached and airy laugh behind "today it's a withered field that trips me up," *kareno ni tsumazukeri.*

鴨渡る
Kamo wataru

月下蘆荻の
gekka roteki no

音もなし
oto mo nashi

水原秋桜子
Mizuhara Shūōshi

『蘆刈』(昭十四)所収。秋桜子は第一句集『葛飾』
以来関東の水を愛して湖沼や河川にしばしば吟行
した。十年後の『蘆刈』は、題名からして利根川
堤の蘆に縁が深い。上の句は、古来東洋画で閑寂
境の描写に好んで扱われた「蘆と水鳥」の図柄を
俳句に生かし、風景と深沈たる心境を重ね合わせ
に表現しようとしたものだろう。こうこうと月が
照る下を鴨がゆく。蘆も荻も音一つない。まさに
水墨風。

Migrating ducks fly

beneath the moon . . . the reeds and

rushes make no sound

Mizuhara Shūōshi

From *Ashikari*, 1939. From the time of his first haiku collection, *Katsushika*, Shūōshi often made poetry-writing trips throughout eastern Japan, visiting its lakes and rivers, of which he was very fond. Much of *Ashikari*, published a decade later, was, beginning with its title, inspired by the reeds along the dike of the Toné River. The verse above recreates in haiku a subject beloved in Oriental art from ancient times, the tranquil landscape of "Reeds and Waterbirds." The natural scene and the mood of deep spiritual quietness frame each other like a double exposure. Wild ducks pass beneath the moon, lit up by its rays. The reeds and rushes are totally still. We might be in a *sumi-e* painting.

とまり舟
Tomaribune

苫のしづくの
toma no   shizuku   no

音絶えて
oto   taete

夜半のしぐれぞ
yowa   no   shigure   zo

雪になりゆく
yuki ni   nariyuku

村田春海
Murata Harumi

　『琴後集』所収。「水路新雪」と題。江戸市中に
引かれた運河のほとりの夜景だろう。「苫」はス
ゲやカヤで編み、舟や小屋を覆うようにしたもの。
「とまり舟」(岸に停泊中の舟)に「苫」の音を響か
せている。しぐれのしずくの音がいつしか消え、
雪に変わっている静けさ。昔の江戸の情趣はこの
ようなものだった。春海は賀茂真淵門の学者・文
人。日本橋小舟町の大きな魚問屋に生まれ、若い
ころ放蕩の余り家産を傾けたが、文才は一世に鳴
り響いた。

Sound of drops

from the docked boat's roof

stops—

the night drizzle

turns to snow

Murata Harumi

From *Kotojiri Shū*. Titled "New Snow on the Canal," this tanka depicts an evening scene on one of the canals that wound their way through old Edo. *Toma*, "roof," was woven matting of rush or sedge used as a covering for boats and shacks. The sound of the word *toma* itself echoes against that of *tomaribune*, "docked boat." The repetitive sound of drops drip-ping from the thatch cover of a boat tied to shore gradually gives way to the silence of falling snow. In winter, this must have been one of the everyday sounds of life in old Edo. Harumi was a scholar and man of letters of Kamo no Mabuchi's line. Heir to a large fish wholesaler's in Nihonbashi Kobuna-chō, he was a prodigal son who almost ruined his fami-ly's fortune, but he was known far and wide for his literary talent.

白露に悟道を問へば
Shiratsuyu ni godō wo toeba

朝な夕な
asa na yū na

漱石
Sōseki

兀々として愚なれとよ
Kotsukotsu to shite oroka nare to yo

漱石
Sōseki

「俳体詩　尼」（『漱石全集』）所収。四行二十四連
の一節。俳体詩は明治三十七年、虚子と漱石が創
始した新体の詩。連句を発展させ、新味ある合作
の詩を作ろうと試みたもので、一人の尼の過去と
現在を、石・子両人が自由に想像しつつ構成して
いる。作家漱石誕生の一因をなしたとも思われる
ような、想像力のはばたきのある作品。上の二行
は漱石が長句・短句を続けて一人で作った部分。
兀々は不動なるさま。尼に託した自戒の語だろう。

Of the white dew I ask the way to

wisdom day in, day out

Sōseki

Its reply: Be but a constant fool

Sōseki

From "Haitaishi, Ama," *Sōseki Zenshū. Haitaishi*, "haikai-style verse," was a poetic form invented by Kyoshi and Sōseki in 1904. It aimed to give a new twist to linked verse, whose collaborative nature it shared. The lines above, both by Sōseki, are half of one verse of a 24-verse *haitaishi* called "The Nun." A kind of free-ranging riff on the past and present of a Buddhist nun by Kyoshi and Sōseki, "The Nun" is such an imaginative work that it may well have been one of the seeds of Sōseki's birth as a writer. The last line must be Sōseki's own advice to himself in the person of the nun.

楽しみ尽きて
Tanoshimi tsukite

哀しみ来たる
Kanashimi kitaru

天人もなは五衰の日に逢へり
Tennin mo nao gosui no hi ni aeri

大江朝綱
Ōe no Asatsuna

『和漢朗詠集』巻下、無常。仏教において「五衰」「天人五衰」などの言い方で知られる無常観思想を詠んだ詩句。生ある者は必ず滅する。天上の快楽をうけた天人さえ、命終の時が来れば五衰の相を現わすというのである。すなわち頭上の華鬘はなえしぼみ、衣服は垢で汚れ、わきの下には汗が流れ、体は汚れて悪臭を発し、わが住む場所を楽しまなくなるという。この天人五衰の思想は後世にもさまざまな影響を与えた。

Pleasure dies

then sadness walks in

And even angels, too, decay

Ōe no Asatsuna

Wakan Rōeishū (Japanese and Chinese Poems to Sing), Book II, Mortality. A poem about the view of mortality given voice in such Buddhist expressions as *gosui*, "the five decays," or *tennin gosui*, "the angel's five decays." All that lives must die. Even the angels who know celestial joy exhibit the five signs of decay when it is time for their lives to end. Their beautiful flowery crowns wither and droop, their robes turn dirty with grime, sweat pours from their armpits, their bodies give off foul odors, and they feel discontented wherever they are. This concept of the decay of the angel influenced later ages in various ways.

("Japanese and Chinese Poems to Sing" is the title as translated by J. Thomas Rimer and Jonathan Chaves in their complete translation of *Wakan Rōei Shū* [Columbia University Press, 1997], though the translation of the poem is mine.—Tr.)

さねさし
Sanesashi

相模の小野に
Sagamu no   ono   ni

燃ゆる火の
moyuru   hi no

火中に立ちて
honaka   ni   tachite

問ひし君はも
toishi   kimi wa   mo

古事記歌謡
Kojiki kayō

　倭建が相模の海で海神に阻止され、荒波を起さ
れて遭難しかけた時、后の弟橘は海に沈んで波を
鎮めた。その姫の最期の別れの歌として『古事記』
にのる。「さねさし」は相模の枕詞。相模の野で
私たちが敵の火攻めにあった時、火中でも私を気
遣ってくれたあなたよ、との意だが、倭建伝説を
離れて読めばこれは農民の恋歌である。野焼きの
火が燃えさかる中で、好きだと言ってくれたのね、
あなたは。「問ふ」は妻問い、求愛すること。

In the little field

of Sagamu, the fires

burned, the fires—and

you stood there among them

and said you loved me

Kojiki song

When the god of Sagamu Sea tried to keep Yamato Takeru from crossing and made the sea so rough that Yamato's ship was almost wrecked, his consort Ototachibana jumped into the sea and stilled the waves. This poem is given in the *Kojiki* as the farewell poem she recited in her last moments. *Sanesashi* is a pillow word for Sagamu. The meaning of the poem in the *Kojiki* context is: "When we met the enemy's fires in Sagamu's fields, even in the midst of the flames you said you loved me." But if read apart from the legend of Yamato Takeru, this is a farmer's love song, and the meaning is: "In the early spring, the fields were being burned and at the fires' height, it was you who said, 'I love you.'" *Tou* is *tsumadoi*, "to propose."

犬の蚤
Inu no nomi

寒き砂丘に
samuki sakyū ni

跳び出せり
tobidaseri

西東三鬼
Saitō Sanki

『今日』(昭二七)所収。三鬼は生前も人気俳人だ
ったが、昭和三十七年六十一歳でのいささか早す
ぎた死の後も、多くの愛読者をもっている。自伝
風な文章に絶妙の味があるのも人気の一因だが、
俳句の方はムラのある作者だった。秀作・凡作平
然と同居している場合が少なくない。これは戦後
まもないころの作。実景と想像を混ぜ合わせた句
だろうが、寒くて、おかしい。三鬼の当時の秀逸
句の一つ。

Dog's fleas

jump off

into the cold sand

Saitō Sanki

From *Kyō* (Today, 1952). Sanki was a popular haiku poet while alive, and even after his rather early death at the age of 61, in 1962, he has continued to attract many devoted readers. The delightful flavor of his autobiographical writings is one reason for his popularity, but his haiku are uneven in quality. It is not unusual to find a commonplace poem sitting insouciantly next to an inspired one. This poem dates from just after the end of World War II. It must be a mixture of reality and fantasy; it is chilly and funny. One of Sanki's best poems from this period.

いくたびも
Iku   tabi   mo

雪の深さを
yuki no fukasa wo

尋ねけり
tazunekeri

正岡子規
Masaoka Shiki

　子規自筆稿本『寒山落木』巻五（明治二十九年
の巻）所収。「病中雪」と前書きある四句の一つ。
この年、子規は腰痛でほとんど病床を離れ得ぬほ
どの重症だった。同時作に「雪ふるよ障子の穴を
見てあれば」があるが、何といっても掲出句が出
色。珍しいほどの大雪が降ったという戸外の景色
を思いえがきつつ、何度も看護の母や妹に積雪の
状態をたずねたのだ。俳句の省略された語法が、
病人の心躍り、空想、あこがれを表現し得て、言
うに言われず深い。

Again and again

I ask how high

the snow is

Masaoka Shiki

From the 1896 section of *Kanzan Rakuboku* (Cold Mountain, Bare Trees), a hand-written manuscript left by Masaoka Shiki. One of four haiku entitled "Snow While Sick." "Snow's falling!/I see it through a hole/in the shutter" (*yuki furu yo/shōji no ana wo/mite areba*) is also good, but the one given here is, after all, the best. In 1896, Shiki's back pain, due to tuberculosis of the spine, was so severe that he was almost unable to get out of bed. A heavy snow was falling outside, the first in a long time, and while imagining what it looked like, Shiki asked his mother and young sister, who looked after him, how high it was again and again. The compressed syntax of haiku is able to express the invalid's excitement, imagination and longing with inexpressible depth.

暗い、 暗い、
Kurai,   kurai,

とわめいてゐる体を、
to   wameite   iru   karada wo,

明るい日のなかに
akarui   hi   no   naka   ni

持出してやる
mochidashite   yaru

前田夕暮
Maeda Yūgure

『水源地帯』(昭七)所収。前田夕暮は壮年期の十
三年間口語自由律短歌を作り、昭和初期の短歌革
新運動の先頭を切って走った。他の歌人たちと違
い、作風を大胆に変えることを恐れなかったので、
歌壇という場で安定した高い評価を得ていたとは
言い難い。しかし彼の自由律短歌には、やむにや
まれぬ勢いで内面から噴きあげてくる要求がある
のが感じられる。上の歌、その意味で自画像のよ
うだ。

Too dark, too dark!

screams this body

as I haul it into the brightness of

the sun

Maeda Yūgure

From *Suigen Chitai*, 1932. For thirteen years, during the prime of his life, Maeda Yūgure devoted himself to the colloquial free-form tanka and led the early Shōwa period movement to reform the tanka. Unlike other tanka poets, he had no compunctions about going through several changes of style during this time, and this daring made it hard for him to establish a fixed position of supremacy in the tanka world. But in his free-form tanka one feels an irrepressible energy welling up from within. In that sense, the poem above is like a self-portrait.

よろこびの
Yorokobi　　　no

失はれたる
ushinawaretaru

海ふかく
umi　　fukaku

足閉ぢて
ashi　　tojite

章魚の類は凍らむ
tako　　no　rui　wa　kōramu

中城ふみ子
Nakajō Fumiko

『乳房喪失』(昭二九)所収。なんという孤独な歌
だろう。作者は乳癌で左右の乳房を切除したが、
あり余る才華を抱いて三十一歳で世を去った。
「よろこびの失はれたる海」とは、うら若い肉体、
また心そのものだろう。その海底で生きながらえ
て凍てついている生物、それがたくさんの足をも
つタコだという影像は強烈な暗示力をもってい
る。タコはすべての足を「閉ぢて」凍てつこうと
している。

The ocean is stripped

of all joy and deep below

the octopus and

its kin, tentacles tightly

closed, will be frozen forever

Nakajō Fumiko

From *Chibusa Sōshitsu* (The Loss of My Breasts), 1954. What tremendous solitude this poem expresses. The author had to have both breasts removed due to cancer, and departed this world at the age of 31, her brilliant promise only partly fulfilled. The ocean "stripped of all joy" must be her young body and the soul itself. The many-armed octopuses, their tentacles wrapped up tightly, creatures barely alive and frozen stiff at the bottom of the ocean, make a very powerful, evocative image.

みづはさす
Mizuha   *sasu*

やそぢあまりの
yasoji   *amari*   *no*

老いの波
oi   *no nami*

くらげの骨に
kurage   *no hone ni*

あふぞうれしき
au   *zo*   *ureshiki*

増賀上人
Zōga Shōnin

『今昔物語集』巻十二。鴨長明、西行、芭蕉らが一様に崇拝し憧れた増賀上人。平安前期に世俗の権威におもねる仏教のあり方を数々の痛烈な奇行で否定した傑僧で、この歌はその人の八十七歳当時の辞世の歌という。ミヅハサスは老いぼれの意らしく、つまりは自分のこと。クラゲは骨がないが、そのクラゲがまるで骨に出会ったような奇跡の嬉しさだと言っている。すなわち仏国土からついに迎えが来て死んでいけるのを歓喜しているのだ。

A doddering

eighty years and more,

on the waves of old age

the jellyfish meets

its bones—such joy!

Zōga Shōnin

From *Konjaku Monogatari*, Book XII. Priest Zōga
was revered and loved by Kamo no Chōmei, Saigyō,
and Bashō alike. He was a great priest, who with
various fiercely eccentric acts mocked the tendency
of Buddhist clerics in the early Heian period to
truckle to worldly authority. He wrote this poem, it
is said, as a *jisei* or deathbed poem shortly before he
died at age 87. *Mizuha sasu* seems to mean "in one's
dotage," in other words, himself. Jellyfish have no
bones, but he feels as delighted as if he were a jellyfish who had miraculously acquired them. He
rejoices, in other words, that a messenger is coming
to welcome him to Paradise and he will soon be able
to die.

中原よ。
Nakahara yo.

地球は冬で寒くて暗い。
Chikyū wa fuyu de samukute kurai.

ぢや。
Ja.

さやうなら。
Sayōnara.

草野心平
Kusano Shinpei

『絶景』(昭十五)所収の詩「空間」の全部。詩人
中原中也は昭和十二年十月二十三日、三十歳で死
んだ。上は亡友追悼の詩だが、発表は十四年四月
「歴程」第六号。雑誌が第五号以後二年半も出な
かったためらしい。筆者は少年時代、これを某選
詩集で読み、詩というものは短い言葉でなんと多
くのことを暗示できるものだろうかと、ひとり驚
き、肝に銘じた思い出がある。

Nakahara, friend!

The earth is wintry, cold and dark.

Well then,

good-bye.

Kusano Shinpei

From Zekkei (Beautiful View, 1940) by Kusano
Shinpei, this is the poem "Space" in its entirety. The
poet Nakahara Chūya died on October 23, 1937, at
the age of 30. Shinpei wrote "Space" in his memory
but it was not published until April 1939, in the sixth
issue of Rekitei (The Road Travelled). Probably this
was because there was a two-and-a-half-year hiatus
between the fifth and sixth issues of the magazine.
As a boy, I read this poem in an anthology of poetry
and have a vivid memory of my excitement at real-
izing for the first time how much poetry could convey with just a few words.

いにしへも
Inishie mo

斯かりき心
kakariki kokoro

いたむとき
itamu toki

大白鳥と
ōshiratori to

なりて空行く
narite sora yuku

与謝野寛
Yosano Hiroshi

『相聞』(明四三)所収。明治三十五年以降八年間の短詩(寛は当時短歌をこう呼んでいた)約一千を抜いて編んだのが『相聞』で、明星派後期最重要の歌集。森鷗外が心のこもった序文を寄せている。寛の評価は妻晶子の名声に対し不当に割り引かれているが、詩人としての気宇は同時代に抜きんでていた。これは、古代の英雄倭建命の魂魄が大白鳥に化し、空高く飛び去ったという伝説に心を託した朗々たる悲傷の歌。

Ancient ages

were like this too

My heart in pain becomes

a giant white bird

ascends the sky

Yosano Hiroshi

From *Aigikoe* (Poems of Love, 1910). This collection, for which Hiroshi chose about a thousand
"short verses," or *tanshi* (his word for the tanka
then) from all those he had written since 1902, was
the most important tanka collection of the *Myōjō*
school in its later period. In his preface to it, Mori
Ōgai bestowed heart-felt praise. Hiroshi's literary
reputation then and now suffered unjustly in comparison to the high esteem accorded his wife Akiko,
but as a poet of the sublime, he was unique among
his contemporaries. In the tragic sonority of this
poem, he expresses his own emotion through the
legend of the ancient hero Prince Yamato Takeru,
whose soul when he died turned into a huge white
bird and flew off into the sky.

何となく
Nani to naku

心ぞとまる
kokoro zo tomaru

山の端に
yama no ha ni

ことし見そむる
kotoshi misomuru

三日月の影
mikazuki no kage

藤原定家
Fujiwara Teika

『風雅集』巻一春。「何となく」という歌い出し
は、気分より事実を重んじる現代短歌では使いに
くい。しかし鎌倉初期のこの歌は、一見あいまい
な言い方も、その使い方によって抜き差しならぬ
一語になる好例。定家の先輩西行も、「何となく
ものがなしくぞ見え渡る鳥羽田の面の秋の夕ぐ
れ」などとこの語を愛用した。鎌倉も後期の『風
雅集』時代の歌人たちになるともっと頻繁に使わ
れる。時代が再発見する言葉の面白さがそこに鮮
やかに見られる。

No special reason, but

my heart stops:

over the mountain ridge

hangs the year's first

crescent moon

Fujiwara Teika

From *Fūgashū*, Book I, Spring. Modern tanka, with its emphasis on fact over feeling, would find it hard to begin with a line like *Nani to naku*, "no special reason, but." But this poem from the early Kamakura period is a good example of how an expression which at first seems vague comes to seem, because of the way it is used, absolutely essential. Teika's predecessor Saigyō, who also liked this expression, had used it in such poems as "No special reason, but /I grow sad/as I look out/over the fields of Toba/ this autumn evening" (*nani to naku/monoganashiku zo/miewataru/tobata no omo no/aki no yūgure*). In the late Kamakura period, the poets of the *Fūgashū* came to use the phrase even more freely. Old words have a new fascination when rediscovered by a later age.

きくときに
Kiku toki ni

わが血は騒ぐ
waga chi wa sawagu

鶏の
Niwatori no

卵を生みし
tamago wo umishi

あとを鳴く声
ato wo naku koe

長沢美津
Nagasawa Mitsu

『雲を呼ぶ』(昭二五)所収。文芸作品の読みには
男女おのずと異なる場合がある。この歌を読んで
思うのは、鶏が産卵後にあげるあの高鳴きを男が
聞いた場合、血の騒ぐほどの思いがあるだろうか
ということ。ここには女性なるがゆえにとらえた
感動の一瞬があるといえるのではなかろうか。作
者は戦後まもなく結成された「女人短歌会」で活
躍し、近年『女人和歌大系』六巻の編者の大仕事
をなしとげた女流。

At the sound, my blood leaps—

the hen's cry

after she lays an egg

Nagasawa Mitsu

Kumo wo yobu (Calling the Clouds, 1950). There are literary works which make men and women read them differently. When I read this poem, I can't help wondering if a man would feel this excited when he heard the hen's loud cry after laying an egg. I suspect the author was able to experience this instant of emotion because she is a woman. Nagasawa Mitsu was active in the formation of the Women's Tanka Association just after World War II, and recently completed the enormous task of compiling and editing the six-volume *Compendium of Women's Waka*.

風花が
Kazahana ga

宙に舞いつつ
chū ni maitsutsu

わが唇に
waga kuchi ni

溶けるひとひら
tokeru hitohira

ひとひらの夕陽
hitohira no yūhi

菅野きよ子
Sugano Kiyoko

『藍青譜』（昭六三）所収。冬ともなると風に乗って雪がひらひら花びらのように舞うのを風花という。夕暮れ時の風花が宙に舞いつつ自分の唇に触れ、すっと溶けてゆく感触を詠んでいるが、溶けたものが風花でありながら、実は夕陽の花びらだったというところが心にくい。「ひとひらひとひらの夕陽」という形容が生きている。表現が透明で、風花と夕陽が二つで一つのものになっているのである。

Windflowers dance

in the space of air

and on my lips dissolves

petal by petal

the setting sun

Sugano Kiyoko

From *Ranjōfu*, 1988. *Kazahana*, "windflowers," is a word for snowflakes dancing in the wind like flower petals. The poem describes the feeling of snowflakes at sunset fluttering in the air, then touching one's lips and swiftly melting. But though it is the snowflakes, the "windflowers," that have melted on her lips, the poet winningly asserts that it is the petals of the setting sun—thus, the vivid description *hitohira hitohira no yūhi*, "petal by petal / the setting sun." With its transparency of expression, the poem makes the duality of windflowers and setting sun become one.

医者殿は
Ishadono   wa

けつくうどんで
kekku   udon   de

引かぶり
hikkaburi

誹風柳多留
Haifū Yanagidaru

　江戸時代の川柳には、一読すぐに意味が通じ、笑いを誘うといった作はむしろ少ない。短い詩型の中で人をあっと言わせる効果をあげるためには、要点をわざとぼかして人に頭をひねらせる工夫も大いに必要である。この句の場合、医者殿はご自身の調合なさる風邪薬の利き目について懐疑的なのである。結句（結局）、風邪を引いたら皆と同様熱いうどんを食い、ふとんを引っかぶって寝るのが一番というわけ。

Sir Doctor himself

in the end slurps his noodles

and crawls into bed

Haifū Yanagidaru

Surprisingly few Edo period *senryū*, satiric haiku, are transparent enough to provoke laughter on first reading. Having at their disposal only seventeen syllables with which to make an impression, they often of necessity skip over the basics, forcing the reader to puzzle the meaning out. In this case, the doctor himself has some doubts about his own cold medicine. When he gets sick, in the end he does best by eating a bowl of hot noodles in soup and taking to bed with the covers tucked in snugly, just like everyone else.

いつしかに
Itsushika   *ni*

天のはら冷えて
ten   *no*   *hara*   *hiete*

をりをりは
oriori   *wa*

われにかなしき
ware   *ni*   *kanashiki*

鳥かげわたる
torikage   *wataru*

前川佐美雄
Maekawa Samio

『積日』(昭二二) 所収。「天のはら」を仮に「天の
原」と書けば、「天の原振りさけ見れば」という
詩句におけるように、大空そのものをいう。しか
しこの歌では「はら」は腹・臓腑の意。「天」も
テンと読まねば歌全体の調子が狂ってしまう。そ
の天の臓腑が「冷えて」というところに作意の中
心がある。冷えた空のはらわたは、いやが上にも
青かろう。青という色は晴朗だがまた憂鬱の味も
する。英語のブルーが憂鬱の意をあらわすように。

Almost without warning,

the belly of the sky grew

cold and now at times

the silhouette of a mournful

bird sweeps over me

Maekawa Samio

From *Sekijitsu*, 1947. *Hara* can be the hiragana reading of the character 原, in which case the phrase would be read *ama no hara*, and mean "the sky," as in the *Man'yōshū* line, "*ama no hara furisake mireba*" ("I turned back to look at the sky"). However, in this poem *hara* means 腹 "belly, innards," and 天 must be read *ten*, not *ama*, or the poem's rhythm suffers. The poem's conception centers around the idea that the sky's insides have grown chilly, taken cold, *hiete*. The chilled belly of the sky has to be completely blue. Blue is clear and pure, but at the same time there is something melancholy about it, as in the English word "blue."

こぼれては
Koborete   wa

風拾ひ行
kaze   hiroi   yuku

衒かな
chidori   kana

加賀千代女
Kaga no Chiyojo

『千代尼句集』所収。千鳥はよく群れて遊び、ま
た飛ぶ。この句は群れて飛ぶ千鳥の中から一羽が
ふとこぼれるように落後し、反転してまた仲間に
追いついて飛んでゆくさまを詠んでいるが、「風
拾ひ行」がいい。見る眼、表現する言葉、いずれ
もさすが北陸に千代尼ありと喧伝されただけのこ
とはある。美貌だったことが名声に輪をかけ、自
作でない句までいくつも彼女の作とされたのも、
まあ有名税といったところか。

It drops behind, sweeps up

the wind and off

it goes—sandpiper!

Kaga no Chiyojo

From *Chiyo Ni Kushū*. Sandpipers often fly playfully in groups. This poem describes how one sandpiper suddenly drops behind, as though falling, then somersaults and flies off to rejoin its fellows. *Kaze hiroi yuku*, "sweeps up the wind," is an especially vivid phrase. The power of observation and the choice of words are no less than one would expect of this poet that Hokuriku proudly claims as its own. The fact that she was beautiful added to her celebrity, and several poems that she never wrote have been attributed to her. Such, perhaps, is the price of fame.

暮れやらぬ
Kureyaranu

庭の光は
niwa no hikari wa

雪にして
yuki ni shite

奥暗くなる
oku kuraku naru

埋み火のもと
uzumibi no moto

花園院
Hanazono-in

『風雅集』巻八冬歌。花園院は『風雅集』撰進の
中心的推進者、自らも一流歌人だった。「冬夕の
心をよませ給ひける」と題する。夕暮れの庭は雪
の光でほの明るいが、室内は逆に暗い。火はある
がそれも埋ずみ火。自分が正座している家の奥は
ことにも暗さを増す思いがする。家の外と内の対
比は、おのずと外界と心の内部の明暗への凝視と
なり、南北朝動乱期の皇室歌人の精神風景をうか
がわせる。

Night almost fallen, the light

in the garden is borrowed

from snow, and inside the darkness

gathers by

dying embers

Hanazono-in

From *Fūgashū*, Book VIII, Winter. The Cloistered Emperor Hanazono, driving force behind the compilation of the *Fūgashū*, was himself a poet of the first rank. This poem's headnote is: "On the essential feeling of a winter's night." The twilit garden shines faintly in the snow-light, but inside it is dark. There is a fire, but only embers remain. As he sits inside, he feels the darkness close in around him. The contrast between outside and inside moves naturally to a sharp focus on the light and darkness of the world outside and of the heart within. You feel you have been given a glimpse of the spiritual landscape of an imperial poet in the tumultuous period of the Northern and Southern Courts.

山ふかみ
Yama fukami

春とも知らぬ
haru to mo shiranu

松の戸に
matsu no to ni

たえだえかかる
taedae kakaru

雪の玉水
yuki no tamamizu

式子内親王
Shikishi Naishinnō

『新古今集』巻一春歌上。春立つころの山家。山が深いので春が到来したとはまだ思えないほどだが、それでも、松の枝や板で作った粗末な戸の上には、とぎれとぎれに、日にとけた雪のしずくが落ちかかっている。松の緑に配するに、きらきら光る雪どけのしずくをもってしたところに『新古今集』好みの絵画美がある。作者は山家のものさびしさを「玉水」の艶やかさによって包み、春の味わいをいわば複雑にした。

Deep in the mountains

too deep to know of spring

sparkling beads

of melted snow fall slowly, drop

by drop, on my pine bough door

Shikishi Naishinnō

Shinkokinshū, Book I, Spring Poems 1. A cottage in
the mountains at the beginning of spring. So deep
in the mountains that one cannot imagine spring
has come—and yet, drops of snow melted by the
sun are falling slowly on the rough door made of
pine boughs and boards. *Shinkokinshū* poets had a
fondness for pictorial beauty and one sees it here in
the juxtaposition of the pines' green and the
sparkling drops of melted snow. With the loneliness of the mountain cottage enfolded in the luster
and brightness of "sparkling beads," another layer
is added to the taste of spring.

作者略歴 兼 索引

芥川龍之介 (1892–1927)　*102*

　　小説家。学生時代は短歌や詩に多く親しむ。俳句は高浜虚
　　子に学び、「ホトトギス」雑詠欄に載ったこともある。のち
　　古俳諧に親しみ、芭蕉はじめ凡兆、丈草ら蕉門の句に傾倒。
　　俳号は我鬼。澄江堂。『澄江堂句集』。

安西冬衛 (1898–1965)　*48*

　　詩人。奈良市生れ。大連に渡り、15年間大陸に在住。北川
　　冬彦らと「亜」創刊。ユーラシア大陸の風土を背景にイメ
　　ージ豊かな作品を書いた。『軍艦茉莉』など。

飯田蛇笏 (1885–1962)　*186*

　　俳人。山梨県東八代郡境川村に旧地主の長男として生れる。
　　早大文科に学ぶが、生家の要請で郷里に戻る。「ホトトギス」
　　の代表的俳人の1人。「雲母」を創刊して、姿勢正しい独自
　　の句境を展開。『山廬集』『山響集』など。

石川啄木 (1886–1912)　*44*

　　岩手県渋民村の生れ。詩集『あこがれ』を出し、一時天才詩
　　人と遇されたが、実生活では貧困と病に喘ぎ、放浪波乱の生
　　涯を送った。生前に歌集『一握の砂』、没後『悲しき玩具』。

石塚友二 (1906–1986)　*212*

　　俳人。小説家。新潟県生れ。東京堂書店勤務を経て、沙羅
　　書店経営。昭和12年石田波郷らと「鶴」創刊、44年波郷没
　　後、主宰。小説集『松風』、句集『百万』『曠日』『磊磈集』
　　など。

和泉式部 (生没年不詳)　*128*

　　大江雅致の女。小式部の母。家集『和泉式部集』、『和泉式
　　部日記』がある。平安女性歌人の第一人者だろう。道長か
　　ら「うかれ女」と揶揄されるほどの恋多き生涯であった。

石上露子 (1882–1959)　*20*

　　歌人。大阪生れ。東京新詩社に入社、「明星」に短歌・美文
　　を発表。『石上露子集』。

一休宗純 (1394–1481)　*106*

　　室町中期の禅僧、漢詩人。後小松天皇の御落胤とも伝えら

POET PROFILES AND INDEX

Akutagawa Ryūnosuke (1892–1927) *103*

> Novelist. During his years as a student he was particularly involved with tanka and poetry. He studied haiku with Takahama Kyoshi, and his haiku were featured in the miscellaneous section of *Hototogisu*. Later, his style of expression moved closer to the kind of classic style that is seen in Bashō, Bonchō and Jōsō's work. His pen names were Gaki and Chōkōdō. *Chōkōdō kushū*.

Anzai Fuyue (1898–1965) *49*

> Poet. Born Nara. He traveled to Dalian in China and lived on the continent for 15 years. Published *A* with Kitagawa Fuyuhiko and others. He created works that were rich with imagery inspired by the natural features of the Eurasian continent. His works include *Gunkan mari*.

Iida Dakotsu (1885–1962) *187*

> Haiku poet. Born Sakaigawa-mura, Higashiyatsushiro-gun, Yamanashi Prefecture, the eldest son of a landowner. He studied in the literature department of Waseda University but returned to his home town at his family's request. He was one of the representative haiku poets of *Hototogisu*. He published *Unmo*, a haiku magazine, and developed a rigorous formal style all his own. *Sanroshū*, *Kodamashū*, etc.

Ishikawa Takuboku (1886–1912) *45*

> Born Shibutami-mura, Akita Prefecture. Though praised as a genius at the appearance of his debut poetry collection, *Akogare*, he struggled with poverty and ill health throughout his short life as a traveler. Just before he died he published the tanka collection *Ichiaku no suna*. *Kanashiki gangu* was published posthumously.

Ishizuka Tomoji (1906–1986) *213*

> Haiku poet, novelist. Born Niigata Prefecture. He worked at the publishing house, Tōkyōdo, then established and managed the Sara Bookstore. In 1937 he launched the magazine *Tsuru* with Ishida Hakyō. Following Hakyō's death in 1969 he took over. Collected stories: *Matsukaze*. Collected poems: *Hyakuman*, *Kōjitsu, Raikaishū*, etc.

Izumi Shikibu (dates unknown) *129*

> Daughter of Ōe no Masamune and mother of Koshikibu. Author of *Izumi Shikibu-shū* and *Izumi Shikibu nikki*. She is perhaps the leading female poet of the Heian period. Fujiwara no Michinaga once teasingly called her a playgirl, and indeed she had many lovers in her lifetime.

Isonokami Tsuyuko (1882–1959) *21*

> Tanka poet. Born in Ōsaka. Joined the Tōkyō Shinshisha group and published her poems and essays in *Myōjō*. Volume of tanka: *Isonokami Tsuyuko-shū*.

Ikkyū Sōjun (1394–1481) *107*

> Zen priest of mid-Muromachi period. Wrote poetry in Chinese. Said to be an ille-

れる。母は藤原氏の出。俗臭を厭い、数々の奇行で知られ
た。81歳の時、勅により大徳寺住持。漢詩集『狂雲集』に
は艶詩も見られる。後世おとぎ話では頓知頓才の僧として
親しまれる。

今井邦子 (1890–1948) *18*

歌人。徳島市生れ。諏訪で成長、20歳の時上京、新聞記者
を務める。島木赤彦を知り「アララギ」入会。女流歌誌
「明日香」創刊。歌文集『姿見日記』、歌集『片々』『明日香
路』など。

上田三四二 (1923–1989) *180*

歌人、小説家、文芸評論家。兵庫県生れ。京大卒。医師。歌
集『黙契』『雉』『湧井』など。評論集『西行・実朝・良寛』
他。小説も多く、歌論から文芸評論まで、幅広く活躍した。

榎本（宝井）其角 (1661–1707) *24*

江戸前期の俳人。榎本氏、のち宝井氏。蕉門十哲の筆頭。
芭蕉追悼集『枯尾花』を門人総代として編んだが、次第に
師風から離れ、江戸俳壇に君臨、独自の華麗な俳風を展開
した。

榎本星布 (1722–1814) *190*

江戸時代の女流俳人。武蔵の人。はじめ鳥酔門、のち白雄
門。芭蕉の句碑を建立し、記念集『蝶の日かげ』を上梓。
同書の刊行を前にして子の喚之を失い、以来消沈の日を送
った。喚之は『星布尼句集』の編者。

王　維 (699?–761) *172*

中国、盛唐の詩人、画家。太原の人。字は摩詰。官は尚書右
丞にまで進んだ。中国自然詩の完成者といわれる。画は水墨
を主とした山水画、人物画で、南宗画の祖とされる。書も草
隷をよくした。

大江朝綱 (886–957) *230*

平安中期の学者、漢詩人。大江音人の孫。玉淵の子。官は
参議に至った。参議の唐名を相公といい、音人を江相公、
朝綱を後江相公と称する。村上天皇の命により、『新国史』
『坤元録』を著す。『後江相公集』2巻がある。

gitimate child of Emperor Gokomatsu. His mother was originally from the Fujiwara family. Ikkyū was known for his eccentric behavior and dislike of the ordinary. At the age of eighty-one, he was appointed head priest of Daitokuji Temple by imperial order. There are some erotic poems in his collected poems *Kyōunshū*. In children's stories of later ages, affectionately depicted as a funny priest of quick wit.

Imai Kuniko (1890–1948) *19*

Tanka poet. Born in Tokushima-shi and raised in Suwa. Moved to Tōkyō at the age of twenty and worked as a journalist. She met Shimagi Akahiko and joined the literary magazine, *Araragi*; published *Asuka*, a magazine of poetry by women. Collected poems and other writings: *Sugatami nikki*. Volumes of poetry: *Henpen, Asukaji*, etc.

Ueda Miyoji (1923–1989) *181*

Tanka poet, novelist, literary critic. Born Hyōgo Prefecture. Graduated from Kyoto University. A medical doctor. Collected poems: *Mokkei, Kiji, Wakuii*. Collected essays: *Saigyō, Sanetomo and Ryōkan*, etc. Wrote widely in genres spanning fiction, literary criticism and poetic theory.

Enomoto (Takarai) Kikaku (1661–1707) *25*

Haiku poet of early Edo period. His family name was originally Enomoto and later changed to Takarai. He was considered the greatest of the ten masters under Bashō. Though he edited *Kareobana* in tribute to his master, he gradually moved away from Bashō's style and developed his own splendid haiku style ruling over the Edo haiku.

Enomoto Seifu (1722–1814) *191*

Female haiku poet of the Edo period. Born in Musashi. She studied first under Chōsui and then under Hakuyū. She built a stone monument with a haiku by Bashō and wrote a volume of poetry, *Cho no hikage*, in commemoration. Just before the book was published she lost her son Kanshi, and was stricken with a grief that stayed with her for the rest of her life. Kanshi edited *Seifu-ni kushū*.

Wang Wei (Japanese: Oi) (699?–761) *173*

Chinese poet/painter of the Tang period. Born in Taiyuan. He used the name Makitsu and advanced to *Shosho ujo* [First Imperial Secretary]. He is known for perfecting Chinese nature poetry. He did ink landscapes and portraits and is known as the founder of South Sung style painting. He also excelled at calligraphy.

Ōe no Asatsuna (886–957) *231*

Scholar and Chinese-style poet of the mid-Heian period. His grandfather was Ōe Otondo, his father Ōe no Gyokuen. Advanced to the rank of Sangi. In Chinese, Sangi is Shōkō. His grandfather, Otohito, was known as Gōshōkō, and Asatsuna himself became known as Nochi no [The later] Gōshōkō. Under command of the Emperor Murakami, he wrote *Shinkokushi* and *Kongenroku*. He also wrote the two-volume *Nochi no gōshōkō-shū*.

太田垣蓮月 (1791–1875) *152*

　　江戸後期の歌人。夫と子に死別して出家。晩年は、自詠の
　　歌を書きつけた蓮月焼を作った。歌は上田秋成に学んだと
　　いわれる。小沢廬庵に私淑。歌集に『海人の刈藻』。

大津皇子 (663–686) *178*

　　天武天皇第3皇子。文武ともにすぐれ、詩賦を振興したと、
　　『懐風藻』および『日本書紀』に見える。天武崩御後まもな
　　く、皇位継承にからむ陰謀に巻き込まれ、処刑された。

大伴家持 (生年不詳–785) *90*

　　『万葉集』中、群を抜いて作歌数が多く、同集の最終的な整
　　理編纂者に擬せられている。繊美な歌風は後期万葉時代を
　　代表する。三十六歌仙の1人。政治的には不遇であった。旅
　　人の子。

岡　麓 (1877–1951) *204*

　　歌人、書家。東京生れ。正岡子規を訪ね、はじめて開かれ
　　た根岸短歌会に出席。「馬酔木」「アララギ」に参加。彩雲
　　閣書房の開業、徳川家文庫勤務、書道教師、書塾経営など。
　　歌集『庭苔』『小笹生』『涌井』『雪間草』。

岡本かの子 (1889–1939) *86*

　　小説家、歌人。漫画家岡本一平と結婚、長男岡本太郎。歌集に
　　『かろきねたみ』『愛のなやみ』、小説に『鶴は病みき』『生々
　　流転』『老妓抄』など。耽美主義的、浪漫主義的作風で独往。

荻原井泉水 (1884–1976) *164*

　　俳人。東京生れ。東大言語学卒。河東碧梧桐と新傾向派の
　　「層雲」を創刊。季題無用を唱えて碧梧桐と別れ、「層雲」
　　調自由律俳句の形成へ。門下より尾崎放哉、種田山頭火ら
　　異色の俳人が出た。句集『自然の扉』など数多く、一茶、
　　芭蕉に関する著書も多い。

尾崎紅葉 (1867–1903) *156*

　　小説家、俳人。江戸の生れ。山田美妙らと硯友社を結成。
　　回覧雑誌「我楽多文庫」を創刊。出世作は『二人比丘尼色
　　懺悔』。代表作『多情多恨』『金色夜叉』で名声をほしいま
　　まにした。

Ōtagaki Rengetsu (1791–1875) *153*

Tanka poet of the late Edo period. Took Buddhist orders after the death of her husband and son. She made ceramics on which she wrote her poems; late in her life, her ceramic style came to be known as Rengetsuyaki. Said to have studied tanka under Ueda Akinari. Her works are strongly influenced by Ozawa Roan. Volume of tanka: *Ama no karumo*.

Ōtsu no Miko (663–686) *179*

Third son of Emperor Tenmu, known for his skills both as a warrior and as a scholar. The *Kaihūsō* and the *Nihon shoki* note that he promoted Chinese. Soon after Emperor Tenmu's death, he was implicated in a plot related to succession to the throne, and was executed.

Ōtomo no Yakamochi (?–785) *91*

Has more poems in the *Man'yōshū* than any other poet. Thought to be a principal editor of the *Man'yōshū*. His delicate style is the best of the late *Man'yōshū*. One of the thirty-six Poetic Immortals. He was unlucky in politics. Son of Ōtomo no Tabito.

Oka Fumoto (1877–1951) *205*

Tanka poet/calligrapher. Born in Tōkyō. He visited Masaoka Shiki and participated in the Negishi Tanka-kai at its founding, then later participated in Ashibi and *Araragi*. Established the Saiunkaku Shobō publishing company and later worked with the Tokugawa family library. He also taught calligraphy and ran his own calligraphy school. Volumes of tanka: *Niwagoke*, *Ozasafu*, *Wakui* and *Yukimagusa*.

Okamoto Kanoko (1889–1939) *87*

Novelist and tanka poet. Married the cartoonist Okamoto Ippei, and had a son, Okamoto Tarō, who became an artist. Collected tanka works: *Karoki netami*, *Ai no nayami*. Fiction: *Tsuru wa yamiki*, *Shōjō ruten* and *Rōgishō*. Her style is aesthetic and romantic.

Ogiwara Seisensui (1884–1976) *165*

Haiku poet. Born in Tōkyō. Graduated in linguistics from the University of Tōkyō. Published a new style of haiku magazine, *Sōun*, with Kawahigashi Hekigotō. As he promoted a style without seasonal references, he moved away from Hekigotō and developed the Sōun style, which was characterized by free rhythm. Among his followers are the unique Ozaki Hōsai and Taneda Santōka. He has many volumes of haiku, including *Shizen no tobira*, as well as books on Issa and Bashō.

Ozaki Kōyō (1867–1903) *157*

Novelist and haiku poet. Born in Edo. He organized Ken'yūsha with Yamada Bimyō and published a magazine, *Garakuta bunkō*. He first made a name for himself with *Ninin bikuni iro zange*. His popularity grew with *Tajō takon* and *Konjiki yasha*.

小野小町 (生没年・伝不詳)　*158*

　平安初期の人。六歌仙中ただ1人の女流歌人。勅撰集入集歌は62首に及ぶが、全部が小町の作とはいえないようである。薄倖の美女として伝説化され、おびただしい小町伝説がある。

尾上柴舟 (1876–1957)　*66*

　歌人、国文学者、書家。岡山県生れ。東大国文卒。落合直文の「あさ香社」に参加。金子薫園と「叙景詩」刊行、反「明星」の旗を揚げた。『短歌滅亡私論』で定型短歌への懐疑を表明。歌集『銀鈴』『日記の端より』『白き路』『空の色』など。

加賀千代女 (1703–1775)　*258*

　江戸中期の俳人。加賀の表具屋に生れる。一説に、18歳のころ、金沢藩の足軽に嫁し、1子をあげたが、間もなく夫と子に死別。不婚説もある。蕉門十哲の1人の各務支考に学ぶ。51歳の冬頃に剃髪か。江戸女流俳人では最も広く知られた人。

柿本人麻呂 (生没年・伝不詳)　*112*

　いわゆる白鳳時代、万葉最盛期の最も多力な歌人で、長歌にも短歌にもすぐれていた。いわば専門的な歌人としての自覚をもった最初の人だろうと考えられる。宮廷歌人として慶弔いずれの分野においても国家的立場で作歌したが、個人的な愛の歌にも多くの秀作を残した。

笠女郎 (生没年・伝不詳)　*74*

　『万葉集』中に短歌29首を残すが、いずれも若いころの大伴家持に贈ったもので、繊細優美な歌や激情の歌など、表情に富んだ相聞歌の作者。家持周辺の女性では一頭地を抜く歌人だろう。

加藤克巳 (1915–)　*40*

　歌人。京都府生れ。国学院大学卒業。中学校教諭を経て、会社経営。「近代」(のち「個性」に改組)創刊、主宰。歌集『螺旋階段』『万象ゆれて』『樹下逍遥』、評論『意志と美』他。

加藤楸邨 (1905–)　*94*

　俳人。水原秋桜子に師事。昭和15年、「寒雷」を創刊、主宰。人間探究派とよばれ、中村草田男、石田波郷らとともに現代俳句に新領域を切り拓いた。『寒雷』『野哭』『吹越』他。

Ono no Komachi (Dates unknown) *159*

The only woman tanka poet among the "six masters" of the early Heian period. Though sixty-two poems in the imperial anthologies are attributed to her, the authorship of some of these is in question. Her life has been dramatized in legend and in many literary works because of her great beauty and misfortune.

Onoe Saishū (1876–1957) *67*

Tanka poet, scholar of Japanese literature and calligrapher. Born Okayama Prefecture. Received a bachelor's degree in Japanese literature from the University of Tōkyō. After attending Asakasha, run by Ochiai Naobumi, he published a magazine called *Jokei shi* with Kaneko Kun'en, in opposition to the magazine *Myōjō* (established by Yosano Tekkan). His *Tanka metsubō shiron* was a manifesto against conventional tanka. Volumes of tanka: *Ginrei*, *Nikki no hashi yori*, *Shiroki michi*, *Sora no iro*, etc.

Kaga no Chiyojo (1703–1775) *259*

Haiku poet of mid-Edo. Born into a picture framer's family in Kaga. One theory holds that she married a common soldier in the fief of Kaga and had a child, but then lost both her husband and child; another authority holds that she never married. She studied under Kagami Shikō, one of the ten masters under Bashō. It is said that she took Buddhist orders at the age of fifty-one. One of the best-known female poets of the Edo period.

Kakinomoto Hitomaro (Dates unknown) *113*

He was the most active poet during the highest stage of development of the *Man'yōshū* in the so-called Hakuhō period. He excelled at writing both tanka and chōka, and seems to be the first person to have considered himself a professional poet. He composed a wide range of poems, spanning works written for occasions of national celebration or mourning as well as personal love poems.

Kasa no Iratsume (Dates unknown) *75*

Twenty-nine of her tanka are included in the *Man'yōshū*. All are love poems written to Ōtomo no Yakamochi when he was young. As one of the most talented poets around Yakamochi, she gave rich expression to her delicate, passionate sensibility in her love poetry.

Katō Katsumi (1915–) *41*

Tanka poet. Born Kyōto Prefecture. After graduating from Kokugakuin University, he taught in junior high school and then began to run his own company. He led and published *Kindai* (the name of which was later altered to *Kosei*). Volumes of poetry: *Rasen kaidan*, *Banshō yurete*, *Juka shōyō*. Essays: *Ishi to bi*, etc.

Katō Shūson (1905–) *95*

Haiku poet. Studied under Mizuhara Shūōshi. In 1940 he began to publish *Kanrai*. His style is known as the school of humanist inquiry. Together with Nakamura Kusatao and Ishida Hakyō, he opened up new ground for contemporary haiku. Volumes of haiku: *Kanrai*, *Yakoku*, *Fukkoshi*, etc.

金子兜太 (1905-) *134*

　　俳人。埼玉県生れ。東大経済卒業後、日本銀行に勤務。加
　　藤楸邨に師事、出征中「寒雷」同人となる。戦後俳句にお
　　ける前衛派を代表して活躍。「海程」主宰。『少年』『蜿蜿』
　　など。

川上澄生 (1895-1972) *112*

　　画家、詩人。横浜市生れ。大正6–7年カナダ、アメリカに滞
　　在。南蛮趣味や民芸風の味わいのある版画作品で知られる。

河野裕子 (1946-) *126*

　　歌人。熊本県生れ。京都女子大卒。夫永田和宏主宰「塔」
　　同人。歌集『森のやうに獣のやうに』『ひるがほ』『紅』他。

川村ハツエ (1931-) *192*

　　歌人。茨城県生れ。茨城大卒業。大学講師。「かりん」「茨城
　　歌人」に所属。歌集『ノアの虹』『孔雀青(ピーコック・ブル
　　ー)』、評論『TANKAの魅力』他。

紀貫之 (872?–945) *202*

　　平安朝和歌ルネサンスの代表歌人。歌合や屛風歌など晴の
　　舞台で活躍したが、官位は従四位下木工権頭にとどまった。
　　『古今集』仮名序は、日本文学における実質的には最初の作
　　家論、歌論として大きな影響力をもった。『土佐日記』など。

岸田稚魚 (1918-1988) *110*

　　俳人。東京生れ。洋品店経営。父、兄とも俳句に親しむ。
　　病を得て療養中に俳誌「砂」を編む。「鶴」に参加。「琅玕」
　　主宰。句集『雁渡し』『負け犬』『筍流し』。

北原白秋 (1885-1942) *200*

　　詩人、歌人。福岡県柳川生れ。詩集『邪宗門』『思ひ出』で
　　若くして明治末、大正初期詩壇の第一人者となる。異国情
　　調と耽美趣味に彩られた作風から、詩集『水墨集』、歌集
　　『白南風』『黒檜』などの東洋的枯淡に至る。童謡、民謡に
　　も卓越。

清岡卓行 (1922-) *214*

　　詩人、小説家。大連生れ。東大仏文卒。法政大学教授だっ
　　た。詩集『氷つた焔』『固い芽』『西へ』、小説『アカシヤの
　　大連』、評論『手の変幻』など。

Kaneko Tōta (1919–) *135*

Haiku poet. Born in Saitama Prefecture. After graduating from Tōkyō University, worked for Nihon Ginkō [Bank of Japan] and studied under Katō Shūson. While he was at the front as a soldier in World War II, he became a member of Kanrai. As a leader of the avant-garde haiku field in the postwar period, he published and led *Kaitei*. Works include *Shōnen* and *Enen*.

Kawakami Sumio (1895–1972) *113*

Painter, poet. Born in Yokohama. 1917–1918 he lived in the United States and Canada. Also well known as a printmaker who worked in a style that combined European flavor with the essence of folk art.

Kawano Yūko (1946–) *127*

Tanka poet. Born in Kumamoto Prefecture. After graduating from Kyōto Joshi Daigaku [Women's University], she became a member of the group Tō, which was led by her husband, Nagata Kazuhiro. Volumes of tanka: *Mori no yō ni kemono no yō ni*, *Hirugao*, *Kō*, etc.

Kawamura Hatsue (1931–) *193*

Tanka poet. Born in Ibaraki-ken. Graduated from Ibaraki University. University lecturer, member of *Karin* and *Ibaraki Kajin*. Tanka collections: *Noa no niji*, *Kujakuao (Piikokku Buruu)*. Criticism: *TANKA no Miryoku*, others.

Ki no Tsurayuki (872?–945) *203*

Leading poet of the waka revival of the Heian period. Actively participated in *uta-awase* and *byōbu-uta*, but politically he rose no higher than Moku-gon-no-kami. His preface to the *Kokinshū*, written entirely in kana script, is the first example of poetic / literary criticism in Japan, and it had a significant influence. *Tosa nikki*, etc.

Kishida Chigyo (1918–1988) *111*

Haiku poet. Born in Tōkyō. He ran his own Western goods shop. His elder brother and father also enjoyed haiku. He became ill and during his recovery began to edit a haiku magazine, *Suna*. He participated in *Tsuru* and led the publication of *Rokan*. Volumes of haiku: *Kari watashi*, *Makeinu*, *Takenoko nagashi*.

Kitahara Hakushū (1885–1942) *201*

Haiku and tanka poet. Born in Yanagawa in Fukuoka Prefecture. He became a leading poet of late Meiji and early Taishō when he was quite young, with the publication of *Jashūmon* and *Omoide*. He explored a style that had a Western atmosphere and a unique aesthetic, and then finally reached a refined Eastern simplicity with his poetry collection *Suibokushū* and his volumes of tanka *Shirahae* and *Kurohi*. His children's songs and folk tales were also outstanding.

Kiyooka Takayuki (1922–) *215*

Poet and novelist. Born in Dalian in China. Received a bachelor's degree in French literature from the University of Tōkyō and was a professor at Hosei University. Volumes of poetry: *Kōtta hono-o*, *Katai me*, *Nishi e*. Novels: *Akashiya no dairen*. Essays: *Te no hengen*.

草野心平 (1903–1988) *244*

　詩人。福島県生れ。中国の嶺南大学に留学。同地で「銅鑼」
創刊。原始的生命感覚を鋭敏に形象化する作品を発表。「歴
程」創刊に参加。詩集『第百階級』『定本蛙』『マンモスの
牙』など多数。

九條武子 (1887–1928) *170*

　歌人。「心の花」所属。西本願寺大谷光尊の次女。九条良致
と結婚。ともに外遊したが、翌年単身帰朝、10余年の独居
生活を送る。才色兼備をうたわれた。歌集『金鈴』『薫染』
『白孔雀』、歌文集『無憂華』など。

窪田空穂 (1877–1967) *72*

　歌人、国文学者。長野県生れ。草創期の「明星」で重きを
なしたが、浪漫的歌風から自然主義を経て独自のいわゆる
空穂調を生む。詩歌集『まひる野』、歌集『鏡葉』など主要
歌集19集。現代の最もすぐれた長歌作者でもあった。

呉　茂一 (1897–1977) *154*

　西洋古典文学者。東京生れ。イギリスとオーストリアに留
学、古典学専攻。『ギリシア神話』をはじめ、ギリシャ・ラ
テン文学、語学に関する著述多数。訳詩集『花冠』。

小林一茶 (1763–1827) *196*

　江戸後期の俳人。信濃柏原の農家の長男として出生。3歳で
母を亡くすなど家庭的には終生恵まれなかった。奔放で人
間味あふれる俳風のうちに、庶民生活の喜怒哀楽をうたっ
た。『七番日記』『おらが春』。

西　行 (1118–1190) *50*

　西行法師。俗名佐藤義清。鳥羽院の北面の武士であったが、
23歳の時、突然妻子を捨てて出家。以後没年まで旅に明け、
旅に暮れる生涯を送った。『千載集』以下の勅撰集に250余
首。家集に「山家集」。

西条八十 (1892–1970) *206*

　詩人。東京牛込生れ。早大英文卒。早大教授。北原白秋、
野口雨情と並ぶ大正期の代表的な童謡詩人であるとともに、
流行歌から軍歌まで、歌詞多数。詩集『砂金』『一握の玻璃』
などのほか、『西条八十童謡全集』、訳詩集『白孔雀』など
がある。

Kusano Shinpei (1903–1988) *245*

Poet. Born in Fukushima Prefecture. Studied at Reinan University in China, where he also started *Dora*. Published many works that gave sharp expression to the primitive sense of human life. Participated in the publication of *Rekitei*. Volumes of poetry: *Daihyaku kaikyū*, *Teihon Kaeru*, *Manmosu no kiba*, etc.

Kujō Takeko (1887–1928) *171*

Tanka poet. Member of Kokoro no Hana. Second daughter of Otani Kōson, head priest of Nishi Honganji Temple. She married Kujō Yoshimune and they went abroad together, but she returned alone the next year and lived on her own for over ten years. She was famous for both intelligence and beauty. Volumes of poetry: *Kinrei*, *Kunsen*, *Shirokujaku*. Poetry and essays: *Muyūge,* etc.

Kubota Utsubo (1877–1967) *73*

Tanka poet and scholar of Japanese literature. Born Nagano Prefecture. He was an inportant member of the early *Myōjō* group, but then moved from the romantic style to his own distinctive natural style, which was known as the "Utsubo style." Volume of poetry: *Mahiru-no*. Volumes of tanka: *Kagamiba* and eighteen other main volumes. He was the greatest chōka poet of the modern period.

Kure Shigeichi (1897–1977) *155*

Scholar of Western classical literature. Born in Tōkyō. He lived for a time England and Austria, where he studied the classics. He wrote prolifically on language and on Greek and Latin literature in works including his *Girisha shinwa* [Greek mythology]. Volume of translated poetry: *Kakan*.

Kobayashi Issa (1763–1827) *197*

Haiku poet of the late Edo period. Born the eldest son of a farmer in Kashiwabara Shinano. His life was marked by misfortune, including the death of his mother when he was three years old. He celebrated the emotional current of the ordinary lives of common people in an extravagant but very human haiku style. *Shichiban nikki*, *Oraga haru*.

Saigyō (1118–1190) *51*

His priest name is Saigyō Hōshi and his real name Satō Norikiyo. He served as a guard at the north gate of Toba-in [the retired emperor's house], but then at the age of twenty-three left his wife and children to become a priest. He spent the rest of his life traveling. Two hundred and fifty of his tanka were selected for inclusion in *Senzaishū* and other imperial anthologies. Volume of poetry: *Sankashū*.

Saijō Yaso (1892–1970) *207*

Poet. Born Ushigome, Tōkyō. Received a bachelor's degree in English literature from Waseda University and went on to a post as professor at that same university. In addition to being a leading children's poet with Kitahara Hakushū and Noguchi Ujō, he also wrote many lyrics to both popular and military songs. Volumes of poetry: *Sakin*, *Ichiaku no hari*. Collected children's poetry: *Saijō Yaso dōyō zenshū*. Volume of translated poetry: *Shirokujaku*.

西東三鬼 (1900–1962) *234*

俳人。岡山県生れ。日本歯科医専卒。「京大俳句」に加入。新興俳句の花形となるが、京大俳句事件で検挙、一時俳句を廃した。句集『街』『夜の桃』『変身』など。随筆にも軽妙な筆をふるった。

斎藤　史 (1909–) *216*

歌人。東京生れ。父の陸軍少将・歌人斎藤瀏の所属する「心の花」に歌を発表。「原型」主宰。歌集『魚歌』『密閉部落』『ひたくれなゐ』など。

斎藤茂吉 (1882–1953) *46*

歌人。佐藤左千夫に師事。精神科医を業とするかたわら、同輩の島木赤彦没後の「アララギ」を率いて精力的な活動を続けた。烈しい生命感を漲らせた処女歌集『赤光』は歌壇内外に広く迎えられた。歌集はほかに『あらたま』『白き山』など多数。

嵯峨天皇 (786–842) *58*

平安前期の漢詩人。第52代天皇。桓武天皇第2皇子。「格」「式」の法典化を推進。勅撰に『新撰姓氏録』『凌雲集』『文華秀麗集』。次の淳和天皇勅撰『経国集』と上記2詩集とに合せて100首余りの漢詩を残す。三筆の一人。

式子内親王 (生年不詳–1201) *262*

新古今時代の代表歌人の1人。後白河院の皇女。戦乱のうちに、肉親のあいつぐ非業の死に遭った。内向する情熱を清澄高雅また哀艶な詠風でうたった。定家との恋愛伝説もある。

島木赤彦 (1876–1926) *26*

歌人、評論家。長野県生れ。小学校長や郡視学を歴任。「アララギ」の指導的地位に立ち、大正期同派の隆盛をもたらした。全心の内的集中を根本とする「鍛練道」を唱え、写生を強調。『馬鈴薯の花』(共著)『氷魚』『太虚集』他。

寂　蓮 (1139?–1202) *174*

寂蓮法師。俊成の甥で、幼時俊成の養子となったが、後に出家。諸国を巡り歩いたが、中央歌壇でも活躍。艶と寂寥

Saitō Sanki (1900–1962) *235*

> Haiku poet. Born in Okayama Prefecture. Graduated from Nihon Shika Isen dental school. Joined the Kyōdai Haiku and was known widely in the Shinkō Haiku movement when he was arrested in connection with the Kyōdai Haiku Incident, after which he stopped writing haiku for a time. He was also skilled at writing essays. Volumes of haiku: *Machi*, *Yoru no momo*, *Henshin*, etc.

Saitō Fumi (1909–) *217*

> Tanka poet. Born in Tōkyō. Her father, Saitō Ryū, was a major general and also a tanka poet. Fumi wrote poems for *Kokoro no Hana*, the group of which her father was a member. Fumi later founded and edited *Genkei*. Volumes of tanka: *Gyoka*, *Mippei buraku*, *Hitakurenai*, etc.

Saitō Mokichi (1882–1953) *47*

> Tanka poet. Studied under Itō Sachio. He worked as a psychiatrist and actively led Araragi after the death of Shimagi Akahiko. His first volume of poetry, *Shakkō*, a work bursting with energy and vitality, was acclaimed by critics and ordinary readers alike. Many other volumes of poetry including: *Aratama*, *Shiroki yama*.

Saga Tennō [Emperor Saga] (786–842) *59*

> Poet of the early Heian period, who wrote Chinese poetry. The 52nd emperor of Japan. Second son of Emperor Kanmu. Promoted the passage of *kyaku* [standings] and *shiki* [system] into law. He ordered the compilation of imperial anthologies such as *Shinsen shōjiroku*, *Ryōunshū*, and *Bunka shūreishū*. More than one hundred of his poems are included in the latter two of these and in *Keikoku shū*, compiled during the reign of his successor, Emperor Junna. One of "The Three Master Calligraphers."

Shikishi Naishinnō (?–1201) *263*

> One of the leading poets of the Shin Kokin period. A daughter of former emperor Goshirakawa-in. Several of her family members were killed in the confusion of wartime. She wrote poems that transformed her passion, directing it inward in a refined, tragic and alluring way. In legend, she is linked romantically with Fujiwara no Teika.

Shimagi Akahiko (1876–1926) *27*

> Tanka poet and theorist. Born Nagano Prefecture. Served as principal of an elementary school and later became a member of the local board of education. As a leader of Araragi, he brought the group to great prosperity in the Taishō period. He set forth a new theory, known as Tanrendō, which focused on concentration of the spirit and emphasized the need for writers to "sketch." *Bareisho no hana* (collaboration), *Hio*, *Taikyoshū* and others.

Jakuren (1139?–1202) *175*

> Buddhist priest. Nephew of Fujiwara no Toshinari. Was adopted by Fujiwara no Toshinari when he was very young, but later left home to join the priesthood.

をあわせもつ巧緻な作風。『寂蓮法師集』がある。『新古今集』撰者の1人。

正　徹 (1381–1459)　*184*

室町前期、冷泉派の歌人。備中小田庄の小松康清の子。今川了俊に入門。定家を崇拝、旧来の歌壇に対立する。門弟に心敬、宋砌らが出て、のち大いに連歌を興す。家集『草根集』(一条兼良序)、歌論『正徹物語』。

菅野きよ子 (1916–)　*252*

歌人。兵庫県生れ。「薔薇短歌会」入会。歌集『藍青譜』。

菅原道真 (845–903)　*84*

詩人、文章博士。右大臣の位に上ったが、摂関家の藤原氏らに排斥され、太宰府左遷、配所で没した。左遷以前の詩文が『菅家文草』に、以後の作は『菅家後集』に収められる。『日本三代実録』などの史書を編纂。

菅原孝標女 (1008–没年不詳)　*34*

平安後期の日記・物語作者。父孝標は菅原道真の玄孫、上総介等の地方官だった。少女期を父の任国上総で過ごし、13歳のとき上京。少女時代より『源氏物語』などを耽読。32歳で後朱雀天皇皇女祐子内親王に出仕したが、翌年橘俊通と結婚。退出するが、再出仕する。『更級日記』の作者。また『浜松中納言物語』『夜半の寝覚』の作者にも擬せられている。

鈴木真砂女 (1906–)　*222*

俳人。千葉県生れ。東京銀座に料理店経営。「春蘭」で大場白水郎、「春燈」で久保田万太郎に師事。句集『生贄籠』『卯波』『居待月』など。

崇徳院 (1119–1164)　*82*

第75代崇徳天皇は鳥羽天皇第1皇子。皇位継承問題から1156年保元の乱をおこし、敗れて讃岐に遷幸。同国で崩御。勅撰集に77首。

増賀上人 (917–1003)　*242*

平安中期の天台宗の僧。比叡山に登って良源に師事。のち冷泉上皇の内供奉、皇后詮子の戒師を務めるが、辞して多武峰に住した。

He traveled all over Japan on foot, and was also active in poetry circles. He had an elaborate style that was marked by a lonely charm. *Jakuren hōshishū*. An editor of the *Shin Kokinshū*.

Shōtetsu (1381–1459) *185*

Tanka poet of the Reizei group from the early Muromachi period. Son of Komatsu Yasukiyo who was from Bitchū Odashō. Studied under Imagawa Ryōshun. He was greatly influenced by Fujiwara no Teika. He stood in opposition to the conventional field of poetry. Together with his followers, Shinkei and Sōzei, he did a great deal to promote renga. Collected tanka works: *Sōkonshū* (with preface by Ichijō Kaneyoshi). Tanka theory: *Shōtetsu monogatari*.

Sugano Kiyoko (1916–) *253*

Tanka poet. Born Hyōgo Prefecture. Joined Bara Tanka Kai. Volume of tanka: *Ranjōfu*.

Sugawara no Michizane (845–903) *85*

A poet and doctor of composition. He was promoted to Udaijin [Minister of the Right]. However, because of a conflict with members of the Fujiwara family, he was exiled to Dazaifu, where he died. Poems and writings from before his demotion are collected in *Kanke bunsō* while his later works can be seen in *Kanke goshū*. He also edited history books such as *Nihon sandai jitsuroku*.

Sugawara Takasue no Musume (1008–?) *35*

Late Heian author of stories and a diary. Her father, Takasue, was a local officer in Kazusa and a great-great-grandchild of Sugawara no Michizane. She lived in Kazusa until the age of 13, when she moved to Kyōto. As a child she loved to read, and even when very young pored over classics such as *Genji monogatari*. At age 32 she attended Emperor Gosuzaku's daughter but resigned at the time of her marriage to Tachibana Toshimichi one year later. She later returned to imperial service. Author of *Sarashina nikki*. She is also thought to be the author of *Hamamatsu chūnagon monogatari* and *Yowa no mezame*.

Suzuki Masajo (1906–) *223*

Haiku poet. Born Chiba Prefecture. She established and managed a restaurant in the Ginza, in Tōkyō. Studied at *Shunran* under Ōba Hakusuirō and at *Shuntō* under Kubota Mantarō. Volumes of haiku: *Ikenie kago*, *Unami*, *Imachi no zuki*.

Sutoku-in (1119–1164) *83*

Emperor Sutoku was the 75th emperor of Japan, and the eldest son of Emperor Toba. When problems arose in regard to succession, he instigated the 1156 Hōgen Rebellion, but when it was unsuccessful he withdrew to Sanuki, where he later died. Seventy-seven of his poems are in the Imperial anthologies.

Zōga shōnin (917–1003) *243*

Heian-period priest of the Tendai sect. Studied on Mount Hiei under Ryōgen. He attended Emperor Reizei and was personal priest/tutor to Empress Senshi. After retiring from imperial service, he lived on Mount Tō-no-mine.

曾宮一念 (1893-1994) *64*

　　画家。東京生れ。東京美術学校卒。昭和44年失明。以来詩
　　作に励み、詩集『風紋』、歌集『へなぶり　火の山』、随筆
　　集『夕ばえ』『海辺の溶岩』などを上梓。静岡県在住。

高井几董 (1741-1789　*140*

　　蕉村門の俳人。京都の人。蕉村没後、蓼太のすすめにより、
　　夜半亭3世を称し、師の俳風を継承。「酒無ければ句なし」
　　の酒上戸であった。『其雪影』『明烏（あけがらす）』『続明烏』などを撰し
　　た。自選句集『井華集（せいか）』。

高橋新吉 (1901-1987) *162*

　　詩人。愛媛県生れ。八幡浜商中退。東京へ出奔。翌年帰郷
　　し真言宗の寺で8ヵ月修行後、再び上京。『ダダイスト新吉
　　の詩』(辻潤編)は、詩壇に衝撃を与えた。近年、禅詩人とし
　　て英米などに紹介されている。

高浜虚子 (1874-1959) *92*

　　俳人、小説家。松山生れ。河東碧梧桐とならぶ子規門下の
　　双璧。「ホトトギス」発行の中心となる。「客観写生」と
　　「花鳥諷詠」を説き、大正後半期以降の俳壇に君臨した。句
　　集『五百句』他。小説『俳諧師』など。

田上菊舎 (1753-1826) *188*

　　江戸後期の俳人。長府藩田上由永の長女。16歳で村田家に
　　嫁したが、24歳で寡婦となる。28歳の時剃髪。その後は女
　　流に前例のない長途の俳行脚の日を送った。書画、茶道、
　　琴をよくした。還暦の自賀撰集に『手折菊』。

高屋窓秋 (1910-) *68*

　　俳人。愛知県生れ。法政大卒。満州の放送事業に携わる。
　　戦後ラジオ東京勤務。「馬酔木」同人。のち「京大俳句」に
　　加わり、新興俳句運動を推進。句集『白い夏野』『河』『石
　　の門』。

高安国世 (1913-1984) *136*

　　歌人、独文学者。大阪生れ。京大独文卒。京大教授。「アラ
　　ラギ」に入り、土屋文明に師事。「塔」創刊、主宰。リルケ
　　研究家として著名。歌集『Vorfrühling』『高安国世短歌作

Somiya Ichinen (1893–1994) *65*

Painter. Born in Tōkyō. Graduated from Tōkyō Bijutsu Gakkō [art school]. Since becoming blind in 1969, he has been writing poems. He now lives in Shizuoka Prefecture. Volume of poetry: *Fūmon*. Volume of tanka: *Henaburi Hinoyama*. Volumes of essays: *Yūbae* and *Umibe no yōgan*.

Takai Kitō (1741–1789) *141*

Haiku poet of Buson's group. Lived in Kyōto. After Buson's death, he renamed himself Yahantei Sansei [III], in imitation of his master's style, at Ryōta's suggestion. As is suggested by his famous statement, "Without sake, there can be no haiku," he was a drinker. He edited *Sono yukikage*, *Akegarasu* and *Zoku Akegarasu*. His self-selected volume of haiku is *Seikashū*.

Takahashi Shinkichi (1901–1987) *163*

Poet. Born Ehime Prefecture. Withdrew from Yahatahama Commercial High School. Moved to Tōkyō but then returned to his home town the next year to train in a temple of the Shingon sect for eight months. He returned to Tōkyō once more and published a volume of poetry, *Dadaisuto* [Dadaist] *shinkichi no uta* (edited by Tsuji Jun), which made a strong impact. Later he became known in the U.S. and the U.K. as a Zen poet.

Takahama Kyoshi (1874–1959) *93*

Haiku poet/novelist. Born Matsuyama. One of the two leading poets of Masaoka Shiki's group, together with Kawahigashi Hekigotō. Played a central role in the objective publication of *Hototogisu*. Promoted the theory of objective sketching and compositions on natural beauty. From the later Taishō period, he was the leader of the haiku world. Volume of haiku: *Gohyakku*. Novel: *Haikaishi*.

Tagami Kikusha (1753–1826) *189*

Haiku poet of the late Edo period. Eldest daughter of Tagami Yoshinaga, who was an officer in the fief of Chōfu. She married when she was 16 but was widowed at 24. She took Buddhist orders at age 28 and then embarked on a long haiku journey, becoming the first woman poet ever to do so. She also excelled at calligraphy, the tea ceremony and the koto. Her volume of poetry, *Taorigiku*, commemorates her sixtieth birthday.

Takaya Sōshū (1910–) *69*

Haiku poet. Born Aichi Prefecture. Graduated from Hōsei University. Worked for a broadcasting service in Manchuria and later, after World War II, worked for Radio Tōkyō. A member of the Ashibi group. Later joined the Kyōdai Haiku group and promoted contemporary haiku activity. Volumes of haiku: *Shiroi natsuno*, *Kawa* and *Ishi no mon*.

Takayasu Kuniyo (1913–1984) *137*

Tanka poet/scholar of German literature. Born Ōsaka. Graduated from Kyōto University, where he later became a professor. He joined the Araragi group and studied under Tsuchiya Bunmei. He led and published *Tō*. He is particularly well

品集』など。

田中冬二 (1894-1980) *130*
　詩人。福島県生れ。中学卒業と同時に銀行員生活。「四季」
同人。詩集『青い夜道』『海の見える石段』『晩春の日に』
など。日本の自然や伝統に根ざしつつ、清新な詩風を追求
した。

谷川健一 (1921-) *54*
　民俗学者。熊本県生れ。東大卒。日本地名研究所所長。近
畿大学教授。『青銅の神の足跡』『白鳥伝説』他著書多数。
詩人谷川雁は弟。

種田山頭火 (1882-1940) *210*
　俳人。山口県生れ。早大中退。荻原井泉水に師事。種田家
破産の後、熊本市報恩寺にて出家得度（曹洞宗）。以来一鉢
一笠の行乞の旅にあって句作した。句集『草木塔』ほか。

炭　太祇 (1709-1771) *220*
　江戸中期の俳人。江戸の人。中興俳諧の先駆者。京に移住
して大徳寺真珠庵に住むが、2年ほどで島原遊廓に不夜庵を
結び、俳諧の宗匠となる。晩年は蕪村と往来し、句に精彩
を生じた。

土岐善麿 (1885-1980) *144*
　土岐哀果。歌人、国文学者。早大卒。読売、ついで朝日新
聞記者。ローマ字3行書きの歌集『NAKIWARAI』を刊行。
石川啄木と親交があった。ローマ字運動、新作能、杜詩の
研究など、幅広く活躍した。『黄昏に』『六月』『遠隣集』他
の歌集がある。

富安風生 (1885-1979) *132*
　俳人。愛知県生れ。東大法卒。通信官吏となる。虚子に師
事。貯金局有志の手になる「若葉」の雑詠欄を担当、のち
主宰。『草の花』『朴若葉』『愛日抄』『米寿前』など。俳論
も多い。

長沢美津 (1905-) *250*
　歌人。金沢市生れ。日本女子大国文卒。久松潜一、古泉千

known for his writing on Rilke. Volume of tanka: *Vorfrühling*, *Takayasu Kuniyo tanka sakuhinshū*.

Tanaka Fuyuji (1894–1980)   *131*

Poet. Born Fukushima Prefecture. Upon graduation from junior high school, went to work for a bank. Member of the Shiki group. He sought to create a new type of poetry based in Japan's nature and traditions. Volumes of poetry: *Aoi yomichi*, *Umi no mieru ishidan* and *Banshun no hi ni*, etc.

Tanigawa Ken'ichi (1921–)   *55*

Folklorist. Born Kumamoto Prefecture. Graduated from the University of Tōkyō. Became head of a research center into place names of Japan, and a professor at Kinki University. The poet Tanigawa Gan is his younger brother. His many original writings include: *Seidō no kami no sokuseki* and *Hakuchō densetsu*.

Taneda Santōka (1882–1940)   *211*

Haiku poet. Born in Yamaguchi Prefecture. Withdrew from Waseda University. Studied under Ogiwara Seisensui. After his family went bankrupt, he became a priest in Hōonji temple in Kumamoto (of the Sōtō denomination). He spent the rest of his life as a traveling mendicant priest and haiku poet. Volume of haiku: *Sōmokutō*.

Tan Taigi (1709–1771)   *221*

Haiku poet of the mid-Edo period. He lived in Edo. He is the main person who brought haiku renewed popularity and respect in the Edo period. He first lived in Daitokuji Shinjuan in Daitokuji [Temple] in Kyōto but two years later got a writing studio called Fuya-an in the red-light district of Shimabara. Later in life he became friends with Buson and composed vital haiku.

Toki Zenmaro (1885–1980)   *145*

Also known as Toki Aika. Tanka poet and scholar of Japanese literature. Graduated from Waseda University. He worked as a journalist for the *Yomiuri* and the *Asahi*. All the poems in his tanka collection NAKIWARAI were written out in three lines, and in roman letters (*rōmaji*), instead of in Japanese characters. He was friends with Ishikawa Takuboku. His interests were broad, and encompassed promotion of the use of the roman alphabet, contemporary Noh plays, and the study of Du Fu's poetry. Volumes of tanka: *Tasogare ni*, *Rokugatsu*, *Enrinshū*.

Tomiyasu Fūsei (1885–1979)   *133*

Haiku poet. Born Aichi Prefecture. Graduated from the University of Tōkyō. Worked for the Ministry of Post and Telecommunications. Studied under Takahama Kyoshi. Within the ministry he dealt with the miscellaneous section of *Wakaba* magazine run by the ministry's philanthropic contributions and eventually took over the running of the magazine. His many volumes of essays on haiku include *Kusa no hana*, *Ho wakaba*, *Aijitsushō* and *Beijumae*.

Nagasawa Mitsu (1905–)   *251*

Tanka poet. Born Kanazawa. Graduated from Nihon Joshi Daigaku [Women's

樫に師事。「女人短歌」創刊に参加。歌集『氾青』『層塔』
他。研究書『女人和歌大系』6巻。

中城ふみ子 (1922-1954) *240*

歌人。北海道帯広生れ。「新懇」「潮音」「凍土」などに参加。
肺癌と乳癌に冒され、乳房切除。歌集『乳房喪失』、没後
『花の原型』。

中原中也 (1907-1937) *38*

詩人。山口県生れ。ダダイストとして出発。小林秀雄、河
上徹太郎、大岡昇平らと交友。生の倦怠をうたって昭和叙
情詩の一頂点をなす。詩集『山羊の歌』『在りし日の歌』で
多くの愛読者をもつ。

中村汀女 (1900-1988) *218*

俳人。熊本市生れ。「ホトトギス」に投句、同人となる。
「風花」創刊、主宰。新聞、テレビその他で特に女性の俳句
啓蒙につとめた。句集『春雪』『紅白梅』ほか、随筆集も多
い。

夏目漱石 (1867-1916) *228*

小説家。『吾輩は猫である』『坊つちやん』などで絶大な人
気をもつ。近代的自我の苦悩を主題に据えた『それから』
『こゝろ』『明暗』など、終始近代日本の根本問題にふれた
作家活動を続けた。俳句、漢詩の作者としても抜群だった。

野沢節子 (1920-1995) *88*

俳人。横浜市生れ。カリエスを病み、20数年に及ぶ闘病生
活を送る。臼田亜浪門下、大野林火の俳誌「浜」同人。句
集『未明音』『鳳蝶』ほか。「蘭」創刊、主宰。

橋　閒石 (1903-1992) *52*

俳人。金沢市生れ。京大英文卒。神戸商大名誉教授。「白燕」
創刊、主宰。句集『風景』『荒栲』、評論『俳句史大要』他。

長谷川かな女 (1887-1969) *208*

俳人。東京生れ。富田諧三(長谷川零余子)と結婚。高浜虚
子に師事。夫の死後、「水明」を創刊、主宰。女性俳句の草
分け的存在である。句集『竜胆』『雨月』『川の灯』など。

花園院 (1297-1348) *260*

第95代の天皇。鎌倉後期の歌人。和漢の学に通じ、仏教の
素養も深い。和歌は京極為兼の歌風を重んじ、清新にして

University]. Studied under Hisamatsu Sen'ichi and Koizumi Chikashi. Participated in the publication of *Nyonin tanka*. Volumes of tanka: *Hanjō, Sōtō*. Literary criticism: *Nyonin tanka taikei* (6 volumes).

Nakajō Fumiko (1922–1954) *241*

Tanka poet. Born Obihiro, Hokkaido. Participated in *Niihari*, *Chōon* and *Tōdo*. She suffered from lung and breast cancer, and had a mastectomy that then became the subject of some of her verse. Volumes of tanka: *Chibusa sōshitsu* and (posthumously) *Hana no genkei*.

Nakahara Chūya (1907–1937) *39*

Poet. Born Yamaguchi Prefecture. Began his career as a Dadaist, and had as friends Kobayashi Hideo, Kawakami Tetsutarō and Ōoka Shōhei. His poems were imbued with a sense of weariness with life. He is known as one of the great lyric poets of the Shōwa period. Volumes of poetry: *Yagi no uta* and *Arishihi no uta*.

Nakamura Teijo (1900–1988) *219*

Haiku poet. Born Kumamoto Prefecture. She contributed tanka to *Hototogisu* and then became a member of the group. She led and published *Kazahana*. She promoted the dissemination of women's haiku in newspapers and on television. She was also a prolific essayist. Volumes of haiku: *Shunsetsu* and *Kōhakubai*.

Natsume Sōseki (1867–1916) *229*

Novelist. Very well known for his *Wagahai wa neko de aru* [I Am a Cat] and *Bochan* [Botchan]. He also wrote *Sorekara*, *Kokoro* and *Meian*, which depict the suffering involved in creating an identity in modern society. In his novels he endeavored to look at the fundamental problems facing Japan. He was also renowned for his haiku and Chinese poetry.

Nozawa Setsuko (1920–1995) *89*

Haiku poet. Born Yokohama. She spent more than twenty years in hospital with caries. She studied under Usuda Arō and was a member of *Hama*, which was run by Ōno Rinka. She then became a leader of and published *Ran*.

Hashi Kanseki (1903–1992) *53*

Haiku poet. Born Kanazawa. Received a bachelor's degree in English literature from Kyōto Daigaku [University]. Also served as professor emeritus of Kōbe Shōdai [University]. Led and published *Hakuen*. Volumes of haiku: *Fūkei*, *Aragō*. Theory: *Haikushi taiyō*.

Hasegawa Kanajo (1887–1969) *209*

Haiku poet. Born Tōkyō. Married the haiku poet, Tomita Kaizō (Hasegawa Reiyoshi). Studied under Takahama Kyoshi. Following her husband's death she led and published *Suimei*. Was a pioneer among female haiku poets. Volumes of haiku: *Rindō*, *Ugetsu*, *Kawa no tomoshibi*.

Hanazono-in (1297–1348) *261*

The 95th emperor of Japan. Tanka poet of the late Kamakura period. Was well versed in both Japanese and Chinese studies as well as Buddhism. He admired

印象鮮明。『風雅集』和漢の序は天皇の作。自筆日記『花園
院宸記』。

藤原家隆 (1158–1237) *166*

　鎌倉前期の歌人。正二位権中納言藤原光隆の次男。母は太
皇太后宮亮藤原実兼の女。寂蓮の婿となり、藤原俊成に入
門。『新古今集』撰者の1人。定家と並び称された大家だが、
対照的な作風で叙景歌に秀でた。後鳥羽院の殊遇を受ける。

藤原定家 (1162–1241) *248*

　俊成の子。『新古今集』撰者の1人。「有心体」を提唱、父俊
成の「幽玄体」にさらに深化をはかり、象徴性の強い歌風
をなした。磨きぬいた技巧は同時代に冠絶する。家集に
『拾遺愚草』、歌論に『毎月抄』、日記『明月記』など。

藤原敏行 (生年不詳–901頃) *142*

　平安初期歌人。父は陸奥出羽按察使藤原富士麿。母は紀名
虎の女。能書家としても知られる。「是貞親王歌合」などに
参加。

堀口大學 (1892–1981) *42*

　詩人。短歌から出発したが、師与謝野鉄幹のすすめもあり
詩に転じた。多年欧米ですごした。訳詩集『月下の一群』
で昭和詩壇に大きな影響を及ぼす。詩集は『月光とピエロ』
以下多数。洗練された瀟洒な詩風の中で人生洞察を歌った。

前川佐美雄 (1903–1990) *256*

　歌人。奈良県生れ。佐佐木信綱の門に入るが、歌風は幻想
的ロマンティシズムの傾向を強く持ち、昭和10年代注目を
浴びた。歌集に『植物祭』『大和』『白鳳』『積日』など。

前田夕暮 (1883–1951) *238*

　歌人。第1歌集『収穫』により、「明星」の浪漫主義に対抗
し、自然主義短歌の担い手として、「牧水夕暮時代」とよば
れる活躍ぶりを示した。外光的な色彩に富む作風だが、生
涯にいくつかの重要な転換があった。『生くる日に』他。

the clarity and refinement of Kyōgoku Tamekane's style of tanka composition, and wrote a preface for *Fūgashū* and a diary written with his own brush, titled *Hanazono-in shinki*.

Fujiwara no Ietaka (1158–1237)   *167*

Tanka poet of the early Kamakura period. Second son of the Minister of the Center on the second position (Chūnagon), Fujiwara no Mitsutaka. His mother was a daughter of the Empress Dowager's courtier, Fujiwara no Sanekane. He married Jakuren. Studied under Fujiwara no Toshinari. One of the editors of the *Shin Kokinshū*. As a poet he is as well known as Fujiwara no Teika, but his style of lyric observation of the landscape is very different from Teika's. He was supported by Gotoba-in [retired emperor Gotoba].

Fujiwara no Teika (1162–1241)   *249*

Son of Fujiwara Shunzei. One of the editors of the *Shin Kokinshū*. He promoted the concept of *yūshintai* ["spirit and body"]. He wrote symbolic poetry that explored his father Toshinari's concept of *yūgentai* ["a shadowy, mysterious and profound world"]. Volumes of tanka: *Shūiguso*. Essays: *Maigetsushō*. Diary: *Meigetsuki*.

Fujiwara no Toshiyuki (?–c. 901)   *143*

Tanka poet of the early Heian period. His father, Fujiwara no Fujimaro, was a court bureaucrat dispatched to supervise the Mutsu Dewa area. His mother was a daughter of Ki no Natora. He is also known as an excellent calligrapher. His work was selected for inclusion in *Koresada shinnō-ke uta-awase* (Poetry contest of the house of Prince Koresada).

Horiguchi Daigaku (1892–1981)   *43*

Poet. He started out writing tanka and switched to poetry at the suggestion of Yosano Tekkan. Lived overseas for a long period. His volume of translated poetry, *Gekka no ichigun*, greatly influenced the course of poetry in the Shōwa period. His sophisticated and witty poems were also full of insight into human life. Volume of poetry: *Gekkō to piero*.

Maekawa Samio (1903–1990)   *257*

Tanka poet. Born Nara Prefecture. Joined Sasaki Nobutsuna's group. During early Shōwa, he became well known for his romantic and fantastical poetic style. Volumes of tanka: *Shokubutsu sai*, *Yamato*, *Hakuhō* and *Sekijitsu*.

Maeda Yūgure (1883–1951)   *239*

Tanka poet. With the publication of his first volume of tanka, *Shūkaku*, with its style that was the antithesis of Myōjō's romantic style, he became a leader of the natural tanka movement. The age even came to be called the "[Wakayama] Bokusui and Yūgure age." His poetry was rich with images of natural light and colors, and his style changed dramatically several times during the course of his life. *Ikuru hi ni*, etc.

正岡子規 (1867-1902) *36, 236*

俳人、歌人。松山の生れ。肺患、脊椎カリエスの病床にあって俳句、短歌の革新運動を推進、「ホトトギス」を発行して後年の俳壇の主流を築き、また根岸派短歌の中心として、のちの「アララギ」の生みの親となる。歌集『竹の里歌』。『病牀六尺』など。

松尾芭蕉 (1644-1694) *124, 182*

伊賀上野に出生。主として滑稽を追求することで民衆化をとげた貞門、談林の初期俳諧を、高度に純粋な文芸へ高めることに生涯を捧げた。のちに『芭蕉七部集』他を形作る蕉門の作品群を指導して作る。紀行文『おくのほそ道』など。

三浦樗良 (1729-1780) *80*

江戸中期の俳人。志摩、鳥羽の人。のち伊勢山田に移る。蕉風に志し、北越、江戸に行脚。京都の蕪村一派と親しく交わりながら、時流に媚びず淡々と作句した。『白頭鴉』など編著も多く、遺稿は『樗良発句集』などに収められる。

水原秋桜子 (1892-1981) *224*

俳人。窪田空穂に短歌を学び、高浜虚子門に入り、清新で印象的な作風で4S時代とよばれる「ホトトギス」の黄金期をもたらした。のち虚子から離れ、「馬酔木」を主宰。句集『葛飾』『晩華』など。俳論も多い。

三橋鷹女 (1899-1972) *194*

俳人。千葉県生れ。はじめ与謝野晶子、若山牧水に私淑。のち原石鼎に師事。立子、汀女、多佳子とともに女流の4Tと称された。句集に『向日葵』『白骨』『羊歯地獄』など。

三好達治 (1900-1964) *28*

詩人。第1詩集『測量船』は、現代抒情詩の展開に大きな役割をはたした。『春の岬』『閒花集』『艸千里』などの詩集において、洗練された近代日本の詩語の世界を生み出す。晩年の『百たびののち』で詩風を完成した。

向井去来 (1651-1704) *150*

江戸前期の俳人。蕉門十哲の1人。儒者の家に生れ、天文、暦学を修めて一時堂上家に出入りしたが、浪人生活を続けた。『猿蓑』を凡兆と共撰。『去来抄』は蕉風俳論中の白眉。嵯峨の落柿舎を営む。芭蕉の『嵯峨日記』は同庵滞留の所

Masaoka Shiki (1867–1902) *37, 237*

Haiku and tanka poet. Born Matsuyama. He suffered from caries and tuberculosis and promoted the revival of haiku and tanka. He began *Hototogisu*, and created what became the mainstream of haiku. As the center of the Negishi tanka group, he established the base from which Araragi would develop later. Volume of tanka: *Take no sato uta*. Diaries: *Byōshō rokushaku*, others.

Matsuo Bashō (1644–1694) *125, 183*

Born in Iga Ueno. He spent his life trying to develop a pure and sophisticated art form from the base established by Teimon and Danrin, who had made haiku a popular art form by observing ordinary life in a humorous way. Later he directed the publication of *Bashō shichibushū* [Seven volumes of Bashō's selected works] and other volumes. Travel haiku journal: *Oku no hosomichi*.

Miura Chora (1729–1780) *81*

Haiku poet of mid-Edo period. Originally from Shima-Toba. Moved later to Ise Yamada. He was strongly influenced by Bashō's style, and had friends in Buson's group. He traveled around Hokuetsu and Edo and quietly wrote his own poetry without being greatly influenced by any of the contemporary trends. Edited many volumes such as *Shiraga garasu*. His later works are collected in *Chora hokkushū*.

Mizuhara Shūōshi (1892–1981) *225*

Haiku poet. Studied tanka under Kubota Utsubo. Joined Takahama Kyoshi's group and with his fresh and striking style brought *Hototogisu* to its golden age, which is also known as the "age of the 4 Ss" (the others were Awano Seiho, Yamaguchi Seishi and Takano Sojū). He eventually left Kyoshi, and began to lead and publish *Ashibi*. Volumes of haiku: *Katsushika*, *Banka*, etc. He also has many volumes of haiku theory.

Mitsuhashi Takajo (1899–1972) *195*

Haiku poet. Born in Chiba Prefecture. She first studied under Yosano Akiko and Wakayama Bokusui, and then moved to Hara Sekitei. She was known as one of the "four women Ts," together with Hashimoto Tatsuko, Nakamura Teijo and Hoshino Takako. Volumes of haiku: *Himawari*, *Hakkotsu*, *Shida jigoku*.

Miyoshi Tatsuji (1900–1964) *29*

Poet. His first volume of poetry, *Sokuryosen*, played an essential role in the development of modern lyric poetry. He created a sophisticated modern Japanese poetic world with his *Haru no misaki*, *Kankashu*, and *Kusasenri*. In his later years, he perfected his own style with *Hyakutabi no nochi*.

Mukai Kyorai (1651–1704) *151*

Haiku poet of the late Edo period. One of the ten masters of Bashō's group. Born into a Confucianist family. After mastering astronomy and calendar research he spent some time as a frequent visitor to the court noble families. However, he eventually returned to the life of a *ronin* [jobless person]. Together with Bonchō he

産である。

村上鬼城 (1865-1938) *70*

俳人。鳥取藩士、禄350石の小原平之進の長男として生れ
たが、耳疾と貧に生涯苦しむ。多年、高崎裁判所代書人。
蛇笏、水巴、石鼎と並ぶ「ホトトギス」初期の代表作家。
境涯詠に独自の境地をひらく。『鬼城句集』『鬼城俳句俳論
集』。

村田春海 (1746-1811) *226*

江戸後期の国学者、歌人。江戸日本橋の豪商、千鰯問屋に
生れる。遊びを好み、いわゆる十八大通の1人。父、兄も賀
茂真淵門。師の没後、江戸古学派の重鎮となる。家集『琴
後集』(15巻)、『和学大概』他著書多数。

村山古郷 (1909-1986) *176*

俳人。京都市生れ。国学院大学卒。教職を経て日本郵船勤
務。「べんがら」「たちばな」を創刊、主宰。句集『城ヶ島』
『華甲』など。『明治俳壇史』など近代俳句史研究に業績多
数。

森 澄雄 (1919-) *118*

俳人。兵庫県生れ。加藤楸邨の「寒雷」に投句、のち編集
に従事。昭和19年ボルネオに出征、帰還後長崎郊外で戦病
を養う。上京後句集『雪櫟』上梓。「杉」創刊、主宰。『鯉
素』『游方』『空艪』『四遠』。

森川許六 (1656-1715) *100*

蕉門十哲の1人。彦根井伊藩士の長男。近江源氏の流れをひ
き、剣術、馬術、槍術の達人だったという。狩野派の絵も
よくした。江戸出府の折、芭蕉に入門。許六の帰国に際し、
芭蕉は有名な「柴門ノ辞」を与えている。

八木重吉 (1898-1927) *116*

詩人。東京府下南多摩郡生れ。中学校教諭。肺結核療養中、
余病を併発、29歳で熱烈にして敬虔なクリスチャンの生涯
を終えた。詩集に『秋の瞳』『貧しき信徒』『神を呼ばう』
など。

edited *Sarumino*. His *Kyoraishō* ranks as one of the best works by any member of Bashō's group. He ran Rakushisha in Saga, where Bashō's *Saga nikki* was written.

Murakami Kijō (1865–1938) *71*

Haiku poet. Was a samurai in the fief of Tottori. His father, Ohara Heinoshin, was also a samurai, and held 350 koku of rice. Kijō was deaf and struggled with poverty throughout his life. He worked for the Takasaki Courthouse as a judicial scrivener. One of the leading poets of early *Hototogisu* ranking with Iida Dakotsu, Watanabe Suiha and Hara Sekitei. He developed his own unique world looking at extremes of human life. *Kijō kushū* and *Kijō haiku haironshū*.

Murata Harumi (1746–1811) *227*

Scholar of Japanese literature and tanka poet of the late Edo period. Born into a wealthy family (a wholesaler of dried sardines) in Nihonbashi, in Edo. Led a dissipated life. He was one of the "famous eighteen connoisseurs." His father and elder brother were both members of the Kamo no Mabuchi group. After his master's death, he became an authority on the classic literature of Edo. Author of many works including *Kotojirishū* and *Wagaku taigai*.

Murayama Kokyō (1909–1986) *177*

Haiku poet. Born Kyōto. Graduated from Kokugakuin Daigaku [University]. He worked first as a teacher and then for Nihon Yūsen [shipping company]. He led and published *Bengara* and *Tachibana*, and produced brilliant examples of modern haiku research with his *Meiji haidanshi* and other works. Volumes of haiku: *Jōgashima* and *Kakō*.

Mori Sumio (1919–) *119*

Haiku poet. Born Hyōgo Prefecture. After writing haiku for Katō Shūson's *Kanrai*, he began to edit the magazine. During World War II he was sent to the front in Borneo; after his return he spent time convalescing. He moved to Tōkyō and wrote a volume of haiku titled *Yukitsubute*. He also led and published *Sugi*. Volumes of haiku: *Riso*, *Yuhō*, *Kararo* and *Shien*.

Morikawa Kyoriku (1656–1715) *101*

One of the ten masters of Bashō's group. The eldest son of a samurai of the fief of Hikone-ii. He was rumored to be descended from the Ōmi-Minamoto clan and was good at horsemanship, swordsmanship and Sōjutsu, as well as at Kanō-style paintings. He joined Bashō's group while in Edo on a business trip. On his return home, Bashō gave him a commemorative phrase that became very well known, "*Saimon no ji*."

Yagi Jūkichi (1898–1927) *117*

A poet. Born Minamitama, Tōkyō. Taught in junior high school. He died from a secondary infection related to tuberculosis at the age of 29. He was a devout Christian. Volumes of poetry: *Aki no hitomi*, *Mazushiki shinto*, *Kami o yobō*.

柳原白蓮 (1885–1967) *22*

　　歌人。東京の柳原伯爵家に生れる。北小路資武と離婚後、
　　九州の炭鉱王に再嫁し、「筑紫の女王」とよばれたが、社会
　　運動家宮崎龍介と恋愛、婚家を去る。「心の花」に参加。
　　「ことだま」主宰。歌集『踏絵』『幻の華』、自伝小説『荊棘
　　の実』など。

山川登美子 (1879–1909) *60*

　　歌人。「明星」同人。歌友鳳晶子とともに師与謝野鉄幹を慕
　　ったが、晶子に恋をゆずる。親の意に従った結婚をしたが
　　夭折。増田（茅野）雅子を加えての3人合著の『恋衣』が生
　　前唯一の歌集。

山口誓子 (1901–) *138*

　　俳人。京都生れ。「ホトトギス」同人。のち秋桜子の「馬酔
　　木」に加盟。第1句集『凍港』は新しい感覚を盛った俳句
　　実践の書として昭和俳壇に新風を開いた。「天狼」創刊、主
　　宰。『黄旗』『七曜』『和服』など。

山口素堂 (1642–1716) *78*

　　甲斐国の生れ。北村季吟について俳諧に入ったが、のち西
　　山宗因の談林風の影響を受ける。芭蕉の往来繁く、親交が
　　あった。博覧賢才の人。俳名も高く、著に『とくとくの句
　　合』がある。

山中智恵子 (1925–) *32*

　　歌人。名古屋市生れ。京都女子専門学校卒。「日本歌人」に
　　入会。前川美佐雄に師事。歌集『空間格子』『みづかありな
　　む』『虚空日月』、評論『三輪山伝承』『斎宮女御徽子女王』
　　など。

湯川秀樹 (1907–1981) *76*

　　物理学者。東京生れ。京大・東大教授。京大基礎物理学研
　　究所所長。中間子の理論的解明により、昭和24年日本で最
　　初のノーベル物理学賞受賞者となる。『素粒子論序説』など。

与謝蕪村 (1716–1783) *80*

　　江戸中期の俳人、画家。画家としては池大雅と並び称され
　　る。漢詩文に多くを学ぶ。印象あざやかな唯美的、浪漫的
　　俳風は、芭蕉の「さび」の詩精神とは対照的で、近世の新
　　鮮なポエジーがある。俳諧句文集『新花摘』、長詩『春風馬
　　堤曲』など。

Yanagihara Byakuren (1885–1967)   *23*

Tanka poet. Born in the family of Count Yanagihara. After divorcing Kitakōji Suketake, she married a rich coal mining industrialist in Kyūshū and became known as "queen of Tsukushi" (an old name for Kyūshū). Next she fell in love with social activist Miyazaki Ryūsuke and left her second husband. She joined *Kokoro no hana* and became a leader of *Kotodama*. Volumes of tanka: *Fumie* and *Maboroshi no hana*. Autobiographical novel: *Ibara no mi*.

Yamakawa Tomiko (1879–1909)   *61*

Tanka poet. Member of *Myōjō*. Like her poet friend Ōtori Akiko, she loved her teacher, Yosano Tekkan, but gave him up to Akiko. She then married someone else in obedience to her parents' wishes, but died while still young. She published only one work in her lifetime, a collaborative poetry collection written with Akiko and Masuda (Chino) Masako, titled *Koi-goromo*.

Yamaguchi Seishi (1901–)   *139*

Haiku poet. Born Kyōto. Member of Hototogisu. He later joined Mizuhara Shūōshi's group, Ashibi. His debut work, *Tōkō*, had a fresh sensibility that opened up new possibilities for Shōwa haiku and for the future of the field as well. He led and published *Tenrō*. Volumes of haiku: *Kōki, Shichiyō, Wahuku*.

Yamaguchi Sodō (1642–1716)   *79*

Born in Kai. Entered the world of haiku by following the master Kitamura Kigin. Later he was influenced by the Danrin style of Nishiyama Sōin. He had a friendship with, and frequent contact with, Bashō. He came to be considered a learned and wise man, and well known as a haiku poet. Among his collections of poetry is *Tokutoku no kuawase*.

Yamanaka Chieko (1925–)   *33*

Tanka poet. Born Nagoya. Graduated from Kyōto Joshi Senmon Gakkō [Women's College]. Joined Nihon Kajin. Studied under Maekawa Samio. Volumes of tanka: *Kūkangōshi, Mizuka arinan* and *Kokū nichigetsu*. Essays: *Miwayama denshō, Saigū no nyōgo Kishi joō*, etc.

Yukawa Hideki (1907–1981)   *77*

Physicist. Born Tōkyō. Professor at Kyōto University and the University of Tōkyō. Served as head of the Institute of Fundamental Physics at Kyōto University. With his theoretical elucidation of mesons in 1949, he became the first Japanese to win a Nobel Prize. Monograph: *Soryūshi-ron josetsu*.

Yosa Buson (1716–1783)   *81*

Haiku poet and painter of mid-Edo period. His paintings were as well regarded as those of Ike no Taiga. His clear and romantic haiku style, which made frequent references to Chinese poetry, had a modern essence that stood in contrast to Bashō's philosophy of wabi. Haiku and essays: *Shin hanatsumi*. Long verse: *Shunpū batei no kyoku*.

与謝野晶子 (1878-1942) *98, 108*

> 歌人。与謝野鉄幹の新詩社に入り、「明星」に短歌を発表、のち鉄幹と結婚。『みだれ髪』で女性としての自らの人間性を肯定し、高らかに詠いあげた。厖大な歌を詠み、歌論、社会評論、古典評釈、『源氏物語』の訳、小説等にも著作多数。

与謝野寛（鉄幹） (1873-1935) *246*

> 詩人、歌人。落合直文門で大町桂月らと「あさ香社」を結んで短歌革新運動の先頭に立つ。東京新詩社を創立、「明星」創刊。鳳晶子と結婚。明治30年代浪漫主義文芸の全盛時代をもたらした。『東西南北』はじめ歌集、訳詩集など多数。

吉井　勇 (1886-1960) *62*

> 歌人、劇作家。東京生れ。「明星」に短歌発表。「スバル」創刊編集に参加。祇園情緒を哀艶にうたった処女歌集『酒ほがひ』で一躍知られる。歌集に『東京紅燈集』、戯曲に『午後三時』など。

良　寛 (1758-1831) *168*

> 越後の名主の長男として生れたが、22歳で出家。大愚と号し、曹洞禅の修行を積んだ。諸所を行脚、晩年郷里に住む。『万葉集』、寒山詩に親しみ、俗事にとらわれず淡々として気品高い歌境をひらいた。歌集は貞心編『蓮の露』。

若山牧水 (1885-1928) *56*

> 歌人。宮崎県生れ。初期の恋愛歌で広く知られるが、旅と酒を生涯の友とし、揮毫旅行もしばしば行なった。『海の声』『別離』など主要歌集15冊。牧水調といわれる愛唱歌では他の追随を許さない。

よみ人しらず *122, 148*

> 歌の撰集で、作者が不明である場合に用いられた語。『古今集』以後の勅撰集に多い。作者名をあきらかにしにくい事情がある場合も用いられた。

古事記歌謡 *30, 232*

> 『古事記』は和銅5年(712)成立。現存するわが国最古の典籍。上巻は神代、中巻は建国時代、下巻は仁徳天皇から推古天皇に至るまでが、歌謡をまじえて記されている。詠み込まれた歌謡は110首前後。

Yosano Akiko (1878–1942) *99, 109*

Tanka poet. After joining Yosano Tekkan's Shinshisha, she published her tanka in *Myōjō*. She later married Tekkan. In her seminal tanka volume, *Midaregami*, she affirmed her own humanity as a woman. She composed an enormous number of tanka and also published many works of tanka theory, essays, translations of classical literature such as *Genji monogatari*, social criticism and fiction.

Yosano Tekkan (Hiroshi) (1873–1935) *247*

Poet and tanka poet. Studied under Ochiai Naobumi. He ran an associated poetry group, Asakasha, with Ōmachi Keigetsu and others and became a leader of the tanka reform movement. Established the Tōkyō Shinshisha, and published *Myōjō*. He married Ōtori Akiko and brought romantic art to new popularity in the late Meiji period. He has many works, including the volume of poetry *Tōzai Nanboku*.

Yoshii Isamu (1886–1960) *63*

Tanka poet and playwright. Born in Tōkyō. He published his tanka in *Myōjō* and participated in the first issue of *Subaru* magazine. First came to public attention with his debut collection, *Sake hogai*, which captured the sorrowful and alluring atmosphere of the Gion. Volume of poetry: *Tōkyō kōtōshū*. Play: *Gozen sanji*.

Ryōkan (1758–1831) *169*

Born the eldest son of a village head in Echigo but became a priest at age 22. Calling himself Taigu, he trained in the Sōtō sect of Zen Buddhism. He traveled all around Japan, later returning to live in his home town. He lived a quiet and writerly life, mainly reading the *Man'yōshū* and the poetry of [Chinese poet] Han Shan [known in Japanese as Kanzan]. Volume of tanka: *Hachisu no tsuyu* (edited by Teshin).

Wakayama Bokusui (1885–1928) *57*

Tanka poet. Born Miyazaki Prefecture. Became widely known for his early love poems. Loved sake and traveling and often went on calligraphic poetic journeys. He has fifteen major volumes of tanka, including *Umi no koe* and *Betsuri*. Bokusui wrote many very popular poems, which were known as exemplifying the "Bokusui style." His style was superb and very original.

Yomibito shirazu [Poet unknown] *123, 149*

A phrase used in poetry collections when the identity of a writer was unknown. This phrase appears often in the *Kokinshū* and later anthologies. The phrase is also used when there is some reason for not publicizing the writer's name.

Kojiki kayō *31, 233*

The *Kojiki*, completed in 712, is Japan's oldest known book. The first volume centers on the period of the gods, the second on the founding of the country and the third on the period between the reign of Emperor Nintoku and that of Emperor Suiko. The entire book contains about one hundred verses. (The term "kayō" refers to the verses in this book.)

日本書紀歌謡　*114*

舎人親王、太安万侶らが撰進し、養老4年 (720) 成立した
『日本書紀』30巻は神代から持統天皇までの歴史、説話類を
記したもので、国史として尊重された。その中に詠み込ま
れた歌謡を言う。約130首。

誹風柳多留　*160, 254*

川柳集。川柳は、江戸後期に発達した俗語による17語詩形。
滑稽、諷刺を旨とした。柄井川柳 (1718–90) の選んだ高点
句 (川柳点という) より厳選した選句集。門人呉陵軒可有の
編。明治2年 (1765) 成立。評判をとったため年々続刊し、2
世以後歴代川柳により、天保9年 (1838)、167編にまで及ん
だ。

梁塵秘抄　*104*

1170年代頃成立。後白河法皇編になる、今様を主とする平
安歌謡集。もと10巻あったが、巻1の一部、巻2全部のみが
現在伝わっている。これに付随する同法皇著『梁塵秘抄口
伝集』巻10には、法皇自身の今様修行の模様が克明に語ら
れていて興味深い。『口伝集』も10巻あったとみられ、現存
するのは巻1の初めの部分と巻10のみ。

Nihon Shoki kayō 115

Thirty-volume work edited by Prince Toneri Shin'no, Ōno Yasumaro and others, completed in 720. Highly respected as a national history book which tells about the history of Japan from the time of the gods to the reign of Emperor Jitō and additional tales.

Haifū Yanagidaru 161, 255

Collection of senryū. Senryū is a seventeen-syllable form of poetry that developed in late Edo. It is characterized by wit and humor. It originally started from a collection of works selected by Karai Senryū (1718–1790) and was edited by his student, Goryōken Arubeshi, produced in 1765. *Haifū yanagidaru* was very well received, and the name Senryū was passed down through the publication of a total of 167 issues.

Ryōjin Hishō 105

A collection of "new-style" songs edited in 1170 by the former emperor Goshirakawa-in. Only the first two volumes (of a total of ten) are now extant. It is interesting that particularly in the tenth volume of *Ryōjin hishō kudenshū* [recordings of oral works], Goshirakawa's training in verse becomes apparent. Today only the beginning of the first volume as well as all of the tenth volume of his *Ryōjin hishō kudenshū* are extant.

著者について

　日本ペンクラブ元会長である大岡信は、これまでに詩集20あまり、文学・芸術論など250あまりの著書がある。「折々のうた」は1979年以来、日本の代表的新聞「朝日新聞」の朝刊第1面に連載されているコラムである。1931年に静岡県で生まれ、東京大学を卒業すると「読売新聞」の記者となる。1965年から1987年まで明治大学で日本文学を講じ、1988年から1993年まで東京芸術大学で日本文学の教授をつとめた。その詩作品は中国語、オランダ語、英語、フランス語、マケドニア語、スペイン語、ドイツ語などに翻訳されている。また、パリのコレージュ・ド・フランスやアメリカのコロンビア大学、ハーバード大学、プリンストン大学をはじめ、各国で日本の詩歌を講じている。各国の詩人と共作した連詩はオランダ語、英語、エストニア語、フィンランド語、ドイツ語で発表されている。各種叙勲を受けているなかに、フランス政府の芸術文学勲章と日本の芸術院賞がある。

....

訳者について

　ジャニーン・バイチマンはニューヨーク市に生まれ、1974年にコロンビア大学から東アジア言語文化の博士号を取得している。著書に評伝 *Masaoka Shiki*（正岡子規）と英語による新作能 *Drifing Fires* があり、この能は日本とアメリカで上演されている。訳書に瀬戸内晴美の『夏の終り』と大岡信の *A Poet's Anthology*（折々のうた）と *Beneath the Sleepless Tossing of the Planets: Selected Poems 1972–1989* がある。NDFL奨学金とフルブライト・ヘイズ奨学金を受けている。アメリカ人文研究基金の研究員（1991–1992）。大東文化大学日本文学科教授、筑波大学比較文学非常勤講師。1969年より日本に住む。

About the Author

Past president of PEN Japan, Ōoka Makoto has published 20 collections of poetry and more than 250 volumes of essays on literature and the arts. Since 1979, his column *Oriori no Uta* has been featured daily on the front page of the morning *Asahi Shimbun*, Japan's leading newspaper. Born in Shizuoka, Japan in 1931, Ōoka graduated from Tokyo University, then joined the *Yomiuri Shimbun* as a reporter. He taught Japanese literature at Meiji University from 1965 to 1987. From 1988 to 1993, he was Professor of Japanese Literature at the National University of Fine Arts and Music. His poems have been translated into Chinese, Dutch, English, French, Macedonian, Spanish, and German. He has lectured on Japanese poetry in many countries, notably at the Collège de France in Paris, and Columbia University, Harvard University, and Princeton University in the United States. Linked verse on which he has collaborated has appeared in Dutch, English, Estonian, Finnish and German. Among his many international and Japanese honors and awards are Officier de l'Ordre des Arts et des Lettres from France and the Japan Academy of the Arts Prize.

About the Translator

Janine Beichman was born in New York City and received her doctorate from Columbia University in East Asian Languages and Cultures in 1974. She has published the literary biography *Masaoka Shiki*, and *Drifting Fires*, an original Noh play written in English which has been performed in Japan and the United States. Her translations include Setouchi Harumi's award-winning fiction *The End of Summer*, and two other collections of Ōoka Makoto's work: *A Poet's Anthology* and *Beneath the Sleepless Tossing of the Planets: Selected Poems 1972–1989*. She has been the recipient of several NDFL fellowships, a Fullbright-Hayes fellowship, and a grant from the National Endowment for the Humanities. Professor of Japanese Literature at Daitō Bunka University, and part-time lecturer in Comparative Literature at Tsukuba University, she has lived in Japan since 1969.

おりおり
折々のうた
ORIORI NO UTA Poems for All Seasons

2000年6月9日　第1刷発行

著　者	おおおか まこと 大岡 信
訳　者	ジャニーン・バイチマン
発行者	野間佐和子
発行所	講談社インターナショナル株式会社 〒112-8652　東京都文京区音羽 1-17-14 電話：03-3944-6493（編集部） 　　　03-3944-6492（業務部・営業部）
印刷所	大日本印刷株式会社
製本所	大日本印刷株式会社

英文書がスラスラ読める「ルビ訳」

The word *rubi* in the phrase "*rubi* translation"
is derived from the name of a precious stone,
the ruby. European type sizes were formerly
assigned such fanciful names, and "ruby"
indicated the small size of 5.5 points. In this
series, difficult English words are glossed in
rubi so that readers can fully enjoy the book
without continual reference to a dictionary.

「ルビ訳」とは？　「わかりにくい単語・イディオム・言い回しには、ルビ（ふりがな）のように訳がつく」——これが「ルビ訳」です。疑問をその場で解決し、最後までどんどん読み進むことができます。必要なとき以外は本文に集中できるよう、実物では「ルビ訳」の部分が薄いグリーンで印刷されています。

- 文脈がつかみやすく、「飛ばし読み」「中断・再開」してもストーリーが追えます。
- 自分なりの訳が組みたてられ、読解力がつきます。
- 基本的に辞書は不要。短時間で読み終えることができます。

46判変型（113 x 188 mm）仮製

講談社ルビー・ブックス

シャーロック・ホームズ全集
（全14巻）

コナン・ドイル 著

小林 司・東山あかね 作品解説

講談社バイリンガル・ブックス

英語で読んでも面白い！

- 楽しく読めて自然に英語が身に付く日英対訳表記
- 実用から娯楽まで読者の興味に応える多彩なテーマ
- 重要単語、表現法が一目で分かる段落対応レイアウト

46判変型 (113 x 188 mm) 仮製

講談社バイリンガル・ブックス （オン・カセット/オンCD） 英語で聞いても面白い！

印のタイトルは、英文テキスト部分を録音したカセット・テープが、また 印のタイトルは英文テキスト部分を録音したCDが発売されています。本との併用により聞く力・話す力を高め、実用的な英語が身につく格好のリスニング教材です。